WOMEN ARE HARD TO FIGURE AND OTHER STORIES

PETER OBOURN

Praise for *Women Are Hard to Figure*

★★★★★ "*Women Are Hard to Figure and Other Stories* by Peter Obourn presents an impressive virtuoso writing performance, including a variety of memorable plots, characters, settings, and points of view... I couldn't help but think of the short stories of J.D. Salinger, especially of the similar reverence for youthful visions of the world... I cannot praise *Women Are Hard to Figure and Other Stories* by Peter Obourn enough. My prescription for readers is take one of these baffling, delightful tales a day. They do what all art must—engage the senses and the mind with wonder and delight."
                    - Jon Michael Miller for Readers' Favorite

★★★★★ "*Women Are Hard to Figure* by Peter Obourn is an incredible collection. The characters have been meticulously created with unique viewpoints and personalities which made the stories multi-layered and compelling. I loved how each story was told from different perspectives as this highlights how the same situation can be viewed quite differently...I thought there were so many subtle but powerful points made throughout which made me ponder the differences between animals, nature, and mankind... A superb collection of stories that will definitely change the way you view and treat others."
                    - Lesley Jones for Readers' Favorite

★★★★★ "Peter Obourn's stories are unusual yet brilliant; they put ideas and thoughts into my head that I never would have imagined if I hadn't read this book. I felt present and was completely absorbed in the narratives... Women Are Hard to Figure is a must-read for readers who seek an inventive, thought-provoking, and emotionally resonant collection of short stories."
                    - Foluso Falaye for Readers' Favorite

★ ★ ★ ★ ★ "*Women Are Hard to Figure*" by Peter Obourn is a collection of endearing stories that examine human nature... intriguing and colorful characters ... The collection skillfully portrays the human character. Each story succinctly explores different relationships and themes that range from grief, aging, family relationships, marriage, and friendship... an excellent literary work with stories that will resonate with all readers."

  - Edith Wairimu for Readers' Favorite

"*Women Are Hard to Figure* is designed to appeal to a wide audience who may recognize their parents, their friends, their lovers, or perhaps themselves within these short stories of seventeen people who navigate their worlds differently... Each story grasps and contains a particular puzzle that invites readers to partake of a piece... Literary short story readers are in for a treat with this warm collection of stories that observe, reflect coping methods, and celebrate the moment."

  - D. Donovan, Senior Reviewer, Midwest Book Review

2021 © Peter Obourn

all rights reserved

ISBN 978-1-7363365-0-2   Paperback
ISBN 978-1-7363365-1-9   Ebook

Introduction by Mike Kielkoph

Cover Art and Design by Molly Fedarko

Illustrations by Molly Fedarko

Interior Layout and Design by Indie Publishing Group

Publisher's Cataloging-in-Publication Data
provided by Five Rainbows Cataloging Services

Names: Obourn, Peter, author.

Title: Women are hard to figure and other stories / Peter Obourn.

Description: Fairport, NY : Ivy Books, 2021.

Identifiers: ISBN 978-1-7363365-0-2 (paperback) | ISBN 978-1-7363365-1-9 (ebook)

Subjects: LCSH: Families--fiction heading. | Interpersonal relations--Fiction. | Bildungsromans. | Short stories. | BISAC: FICTION / Short Stories (single author) | FICTION / Literary.

Classification: LCC PS3615.B68 W66 2021 (print) | LCC PS3615.B68 (ebook) | DDC 813/.6--dc23.

For Linda

ACKNOWLEDGMENTS

I would like to thank my *Women Are Hard to Figure* team: my cover artist/daughter Molly Fedarko, my book designer and typographer Danielle Smith-Boldt, my marketing man Martyn Beeny, my proofreader/editor Mike Kielkoph and Chrissy Hobbs of Indie Publishing Group for the interior layout and design. Finally, thanks to the team at Aaxel Author Services for their publishing and marketing assistance.

There are many, many writers who helped me over the years, and I thank them all. It's impossible to even list them without having it look like I've started another book, but I'd like to single out a few. I thank Steve Heller, who led the first writing seminar I attended, who convinced me my work is publishable. He even invited me to Kansas State to share my work with one of his classes. And Christina Shea, my mentor at Lesley University who taught me how to write a scene. Only after Christina's guidance did my writing grow wings of its own. And all the rest of the faculty of writers at the wonderful, intimate Lesley University MFA Program, who all take time for individual tutoring, especially Michael Lowenthal, and Suzanne Berne. And Nancy Zafris, who taught me that you have to read and reread and write and rewrite until you find it. And the late, great master teacher Lee Abbot who taught us to keep the Mennonites out of the story unless they belong there (usually, they don't) and Curtis Sittenfeld who introduced me to her agent (who was, unfortunately, not overwhelmed by my work) and all the tireless leaders of the Old Forge Writers Workshop that I have attended for over 20 years and Karen Novak who led our short-lived Adirondack Writers Group. I still get questions whenever I wear my Novak University sweatshirt. And my writer/brother Ted who reads with a gimlet eye and my sister/publisher Mike who can find a typo in a haystack. and all my writer's group friends and readers who have actually read and praised my work with seldom a discouraging word.

CONTENTS

FOREWORD

"My dad had eight fingers. My mother was beautiful. My brother Sam was trying to figure out where dreams come from." Who cares? I'm confident you will as you read "An Artist in the Family," the first of seventeen entries in this eclectic series. You'll see yourself, your relatives, your friends, and your colleagues in the characters and their circumstances. You'll laugh, you'll cry, and you'll wonder about a lot of things, including how Ned the goldfish could read the newspaper, hit a game-winning home run, and grow a mustache. But once you've read "The Goldfish with Long Black Hair" you'll understand all those things—and a whole lot more.

That's why it was such a joy to edit this collection of Peter Obourn's stories and why I was so excited to tell you about them, including "The Birds of Bristol Court" where you'll meet many provocative people and ponder their perplexing relationships. And that ain't no bull. But the next story is.

You'll meet a two-ton animal in "The Bull" who, they say, looks fearsome and *"sees what he sees and knows what he knows."* After reading the story, you'll see what you see and know what you know in ways you never did before.

"Until I found the box in the attic, I thought my mother was just the best car saleswoman in Park City." If you think you know your parents, you might need to think again. Find out why in "Circus City."

Then there's the intriguing "Marilee," who had never had a date, and Flora who, in "Scenes from a Widower's Life," shows up in a dress—to go fishing.

In "Edith's Summer" you'll meet Albert "the cow" and consider old generational relationships from new perspectives. Then you'll explore, in uncommon ways, the common concern of what makes a house a home in "Ghosts in the House"

"I was stripped naked and told I was the chief suspect because they never found my rifle. I told them I never owned a rifle. Knowing I was innocent but would be sent to solitary anyway, I trembled, but there was no other choice." And there's no other choice for you either if you're looking for memorable short stories like "The Liberation" where you'll examine the fine line between sanity and insanity.

"It's difficult to say this without sounding like I'm bragging, but as with many great lovers, I started early. My first conquest transpired in the summer of 1954 when I was a mere thirteen years old." Live those days along with

Tommy, Irene, Tony, and the gang in "Women are Hard to Figure."

You'll never forget the filmmaker or the night watch-man, Cindy or the pool boy, Kaplan's Furniture Store, Morgan the plumber, the inmate, the professor, the kids, the senior citizens, the goldfish, blind Mr. Bemis who could find every record in his store, and the many other compelling characters and captivating situations offered in a variety of cinematic styles.

Obourn's stories reflect empathy and insight, from the unbridled imaginations of children to the unimag-inable detachment of dementia, from love and sacrifice to fate and uncommon sense, so if you're like me, you won't merely read these memorable stories, you'll live them.

— Mike Kielkopf
Mesa, Arizona
January 6, 2021

AN ARTIST IN THE FAMILY

WE lived in a small town.

My dad had eight fingers.

My mother was beautiful.

My brother Sam was trying to figure out where dreams come from.

We were sitting around the kitchen table and having a family meeting. Sam, somehow, had managed to flunk eighth grade—every course except art. Sam wasn't that bad a student, although school officials did commonly refer to him as "challenged." And Sam did have some problems. The school said Sam had ADD and ADHD and all those acronyms for things that give kids unlimited time on tests and other privileges. But he had been doing okay.

"How could you flunk everything?" Dad asked. "How could you flunk physical education? No one flunks gym."

"I didn't flunk everything," Sam said. "I got an A in art."

"Don't you want to be smart like your brother, get good grades, go to college?"

"No, not really."

"It's okay, Sammy," said my mother. "You try hard."

"It's not okay," said Dad. "No son of mine is going to work in the car shops." He held up his hands to show that he was missing his right index finger and his left pinkie, lost to the cables on the overhead hoists on two separate occasions. The car shops made railroad cars. It was the only industry in town—dirty, noisy, dangerous, and unhealthy. Both our grandfathers had worked in the car shops. One had died at age fifty in an assembly line accident and the other of emphysema caused simply by breathing at work for thirty years.

Mom just sat and smiled at Sam. I didn't say anything. "Pops," said Sam, "I'm going to be an artist."

Dad gazed at me and then at the ceiling. Then he stared at Mom, who stared back. Finally, his gaze returned to Sam. "That's good," said Dad. "That's okay; you be an artist. You be whatever you want to be. But things are going to have to change, right, Sam?" And he ruffled Sam's hair as he said it.

"How could you flunk gym?" I asked that night as soon as we were in bed. Sam and I shared a room in our two-bedroom house.

"I just didn't show up, that's how. I was getting special

help in art. And you know what? Some days we went in a canoe that's hidden down by the creek."

"You went canoeing with a teacher?"

"Yeah, a few times," Sam said as if it was nothing. "We took our sketch pads."

The junior high art teacher, Miss Mirabell, was pretty and young—twenty-five at the most. I was lying in bed, listening to my little brother, picturing him and the beautiful Miss Mirabell going to sea in a pea-green boat. And she gave him an A? I was instantly jealous. "What on earth could you two talk about?" I asked. "You're fourteen. She's at least ten years older than you. She's your teacher." Now, if Miss Mirabell was in love with *me*, that would be something else. After all, I was much older than Sam.

"Not *her*, you dummy, *him*—Mr. Ambrosia, the high school art teacher. Miss Mirabell has me working with him during gym class."

"Sam," I said, "not Mr. Ambrosia. He lives with another man. Do you understand what that means? And you're going off in the woods with *him?*"

It was quiet for a full minute. Then Sam said, "Bill, I know I'm only fourteen, but I'm well aware that Mr. Ambrosia is gay, and I'm also aware that you and your pals seem to find that hilarious. Now, what I want you to tell me is what that has to do with anything. So please just shut up."

Our parents met with the principal as the school

year was about to end. There was no way around it. Sam would have to repeat eighth grade.

We had a dining room, but we never ate there. It was the study room for Sam and me, and the dining room table was piled high with our school books and papers. I was studying calculus, and Sam had a history book open on the table when he called me to the back window. The trees in our yard had turned bright yellow and red. We lived on Walnut Street, but I knew the trees were maples. I couldn't believe the summer was gone, and we were already back in school.

Washday wasn't necessarily Monday. Instead, it was whatever day the wind was right so the soot from the car shop chimneys wouldn't drift onto the laundry that had been hung out to dry. Mom, an expert weather forecaster out of necessity and experience, was hanging the sheets. She would reach up, pull the clothesline down, fold the edge of a sheet over it, take a clothespin from her teeth, and push it down to hold the sheet in place. The wind blowing the car shop soot away was blowing her hair and pushing her blue housedress tight around her still slim waist. The damp sheet was almost touching the ground, so she bent down and hooked a thin, weathered clothesline pole with its rusty hook under the line to raise the sheet more than a foot above the green grass. As she reached for the next sheet, the one on the line billowed and cracked in the wind like a whip.

"That's where dreams come from," said Sam.

"What?" I said.

"Dreams come from the things we see and things we hear that make an impression on us. Maybe we don't even know it—like this scene."

"What scene?" I said. "You mean Mom hanging laundry?"

"Yeah," he said. "Exactly. Mom hanging laundry, a scene that shows what it's like to live in a town like this." I glanced once more. By then there were four sheets flapping gracefully, testing the thin, gray clothesline poles. Mom's blue housedress stood out against the backdrop of the red maple next to the back fence. As I glanced down at the table, next to Sam's history book I noticed several pencil sketches of billowing bed sheets.

About a week later, Sam and I were again sitting at the dining room table. I was writing an essay on the Renaissance when I noticed Sam was staring at a single piece of paper from the many scattered around him. I could make out some with scribbles, some with cartoons, and others with pictures and blobs. He was poking at that single paper, attacking it, gesturing at it, just fooling around. He held a red crayon in his right hand and sported a red crayon mark on his cheek.

"Sam," I said, "listen to me. If you really want to be an artist, you have to work at it. And you need to focus, at least some of the time, on your other classes."

He didn't even look up. He just kept playing with his crayon. "This is everything," he said.

"No, Sam. Look at Michelangelo's *David*. You think he did that with crayons? How about the Sistine Chapel? Did he just poke at it the way you're doing?"

Sam carefully put his crayon down. "No, he didn't, but, well, I think maybe you're confusing art and craft. The craft part is important. I'll learn that. That will be hard. I understand that. But art is something different, something more."

I didn't know what he was talking about, but he was smiling. "Take your pencil and draw a circle," he said. "Go ahead. Try hard. Make it as good as you can. Any size." It only took me about two minutes, and it was pretty good. When I finished, I held it up for him to see. Sam then took his red crayon, peered at me, closed his eyes and, in one second, drew a circle with nothing but a flick of his wrist. It was perfect.

The next day I was still working on my Renaissance report when Sam brought a folder into the dining room and set it down next to me. "Mom saved these. This is our best work, yours and mine. This one is mine. I was seven." It said "DAD" in black crayon and was signed "Sam" in red crayon. It showed a man with dots for eyes standing in front of a huge, dark factory with smokestacks belching. The man was clean and bright as if the sun were shining on him. Dad didn't have eight fingers. He didn't have any fingers. And instead of hands, he had pink circles at the ends of his arms.

Sam left the folder on the table. I stared at the picture I had drawn and that Mom had saved. It said "MOTHER." Her hands looked like claws.

Then there was another crisis. A letter arrived that said Sam had ten unexcused absences from gym, and it was only the middle of October.

"You need to talk to the principal," Mom told Dad.

Sam said not to do anything or someone else might get into trouble. "Who?" asked Dad.

"Well," said Sam, "maybe Miss Mirabell."

"Who?" Dad asked again.

"My art teacher."

"Dad," I said, "I'm thinking of taking an art course next semester."

"You, Bill? But you're taking science and math. You're going to college."

"I am," I said. "So did Miss Mirabell. Art is really important, Dad. If I get an A in art, that will mean a lot on my college applications."

That night Sam asked me, "Are you really going to take a course from Mr. Ambrosia?"

"Yeah," I said, "I am."

"Better watch out. I hear he likes soccer players."

"Shut up," I said.

So Dad, with a new interest in art, visited Miss Mirabell at school. "A nice young lady," said Dad. "Smart." He spread his eight fingers on the kitchen table. "She said she'd talk to the gym teacher, and it would be no problem. But I think we need to talk to the principal." Then Dad started to stand.

"Wait," Sam said. "I need to show you something, Pops."

On that particular October day, sunny and beautiful, the trees were at their peak of autumn color. Sam insisted I go along. It was a long walk, halfway across town. Sam took Dad and me down the steep hill to the valley where the creek runs past the dump. "Why are we at the creek?" asked Dad. Sam didn't answer. We traipsed through the tall grass and weeds along the creek's edge. There, hidden in some bushes, was a canoe and two beat-up paddles. Before Dad could say anything, Sam said, "Pops, don't ask me anymore. Don't ask about the canoe or about Miss Mirabell. Just watch and listen. Please?"

"Are you sure this is a good idea?" I whispered to Sam.

"I don't know," he said. "I just know I have to show this to Dad."

Dad stood just stood there staring at the creek until he finally said, "I can't swim."

Sam, without taking off his shoes or rolling up his

pants, stepped into the water and waded to the middle of the creek. The water only came up to his knees. "See. It's just a creek," he said. "It's only a foot deep." Sam and I took the paddles, me in the back, and Dad sat in the middle. "Just sit still," Sam said. "Trust me, Pops." With that encouragement, Dad's death grip on the gunnel relaxed a bit. We floated down the creek, past the dump, and then around the first bend. The creek wound its way around the edge of the village and eventually found its way to the river. There were other villages and towns around us—suburban sprawl—but we couldn't see any of that during the whole afternoon in the canoe. We never saw a road or a house or even a tended field—only the natural world the creek meandered through. We barely got the paddles wet, preferring to let the current carry us slowly. Autumn leaves and random sticks passed us by, so it seemed we were moving even more slowly because the current was faster than the canoe's progress.

Even though the water was flowing, the surface was as placid as a black mirror, but we could see only a partial reflection. Beyond that looking glass we could view the blades of the green grass on the bottom of the creek waving in the current. The water reflected a black sky dotted by white clouds. The sun was high, the trees reflected in the water, and the sunlight bounced back onto their overhanging branches as they shimmered with the reflected light. The banks were covered in red sand-stone and bedrock, so an earth-toned world of greens and ochre and browns reflected crookedly back to us as we floated through it.

The quiet was so natural that I began to listen to the leaves in the trees and the drone of insects, a continuum under the occasional chatter of the squirrels and birdsong. Our paddles occasionally sliced almost silently through the water and, at times, we could even hear the tiny insects darting across the water.

As we rounded a bend, we found ourselves in a pond in the middle of the creek. A fish jumped, but we didn't see it. We did see the circle of the splash and the concentric circles moving outward—then we noticed something huge in the water. We looked up. It was the reflection of a massive oak tree standing alone as if it had cleared the area around itself by its own power, a perfect circle of tangled branches and leaves.

The oak leaves had turned a deep reddish-brown. Only a few had fallen, but the others were ready to take the leap. A gust released many of the giant tree's leaves, and they swirled and floated groundward in slow motion. Many of them landed weightlessly on the water and floated along with us.

As Sam turned the canoe slowly toward home he said, "Pops, this is a song we are in—a song about us, about the pond, about the water, and about what is happening now. Can you feel it? Can you see it?"

"I'm trying, Sam," said Dad. "I'm trying. Honest I am."

"Don't try," said Sam. "Just feel it." And as we slid into the shore he added, "Don't worry, Pops. It's okay. The world is a song. You'll feel it."

We stashed the canoe and headed home in silence.

At dinner nothing was said about our voyage. Dad reached across the table, took Mom's hand, and announced that he had decided not to meet with the principal. "What good would it do? Miss Mirabell is a nice young lady."

"Pops," said Sam, "I figured out today that dreams and art come from the same place."

"How's that?"

"I don't really know, Pops, someplace inside us, somehow, but when they come, they *mean* something and they, they...I don't know how they do it, but they grab us. You know, they demand attention. You know what I mean, Pops?" Dad stared at Sam but didn't say anything. "Pops?" said Sam.

"I'm trying," said Dad.

I left them, moved into the dining room, picked up a pencil and my Renaissance notes, went outside, and sat on the back steps. I turned a sheet over and tried to draw a few circles, the maple tree, the back fence, a cloud lit by the late afternoon sun.

THE BIRDS OF BRISTOL COURT

Flora

THE widow Florrine Smythe, who preferred to be called Flora, but not Flo, lived at 16 Bristol Court.

Flora sat on the stool in front of her dressing table, feeling her bottom spill over just a little on the sides. Once she had finished her facial work, she would carefully squeeze herself into her foundation garment that worked in a ruthless and primitive way by pushing a lot of her upward in a flattering manner. The problem was that when she wore it she could barely breathe and was forced to sit on the edge of the furniture. Three hours was about all she could take. She knew the solution was to lose fifteen pounds, and every time she put the damn garment on she committed to doing exactly that, but once she escaped the garment, and meal time (or between-meal time) arrived, her resolve melted in the face of temptation.

Mildred

The young widow, Mildred Forsythe, lived next door at 18 Bristol Court in a house that, at first glance, mirrored Flora's but, on closer examination, was a little finer in every tasteful detail.

Mildred, who was seldom called Millie, was seated in her living room, trying to focus on a needlepoint pillow cover. Every few minutes she walked to the front window, parted the drapes a fraction of an inch, and peered into the street.

On her fifteenth trip, her vigil was rewarded. A car pulled into Flora's driveway and disappeared as the garage door was raised and lowered to allow the car to slip into a vacant spot. Mildred knew the car, having seen that performance many times. It belonged to Lucia Fiorini, one of the kitchen staff at the country club who delivered meals that Flora would heat up and pass off as her own with much theatrical detail. Mildred told her friend Betty that Flora would have made the perfect television chef—if only she knew how to cook.

Mildred knew with certainty that around six o'clock she would see Harold Overmeyer emerge from his house dressed for an evening at Flora's. He would never be unfashionably early, but likewise, he dared not be late.

Harry

Harold Overmeyer, a widower, lived at 17 Bristol Court, almost directly across the street from Flora and Mildred; he was indifferent to the subtle differences between the widows' houses.

Harry was watching the Giants-Steelers game that had gone into overtime. He glanced at his watch. He was due at Flora's in twenty minutes for cocktails, and he knew from experience he would not get his second drink if he were late. Flora would rush him right to dinner, thereby upsetting the flow of his entire evening. But an evening with Flora required at least two manhattans. He felt so awkward around intelligent women. He wished Joan were there to steady him, which was absurd; the only reason he was with this woman was because Joan was gone.

He was going to miss the game's tense, sudden-death ending. He still had to shower, shave, and dress. He amended the budgeted time for his toilet from fifteen to ten minutes. He wished he had listened more carefully to his son Jeffery who had shown him how to record a program in progress. He stared at the remote and its fifty tiny buttons. He hesitated, and then, afraid if he pushed the wrong button the whole system would self-destruct, gave up, sighed, pushed "Off," and headed for the shower.

At 6:01 p.m., Harry combed the few hairs left on his head and hurried across the street. He glanced up at Mildred's front window but did not see her because, except for one eyeball, she was concealed behind closed drapery.

Dinner

Flora was stiffly perched on the edge of the sofa trying to breathe more or less naturally. Harry was deep in the wing chair that must have been the favorite of her late husband, Charles, whose portraits at every stage of advancing age and weight were scattered around the house.

"Shall we eat?" asked Flora brightly.

"Sure, Flora," said Harry, smiling, "but let's have just one more short one."

Flora left Harry to make the drinks while she went to the kitchen and pretended to put the finishing touches on the meal. She stirred and tasted, wondering how she could get Harry off the subject of his grandson Zeke. "A good kick in the pants—that's what he needs," Harry had said at least three times, and she knew the repetition would increase with the second manhattan. He never had more than two, and then a glass of wine or two. She could live with that. At the right level of alcohol he was a delight, but it was a narrow band.

Harry joined her in the kitchen, handed her a fresh drink, and moved to the window. "Had a terrible drive today on that hole," he said, pointing across the cart path to the golf course. "Sliced it over the rough, ended up somewhere over there, I think, in Mildred's bushes. Out of bounds—a new four-dollar Titleist."

Flora, shuffling to his side, could not imagine a more boring subject than golf, so she said, "It doesn't look that bad, does it? Can you imagine that thing could cause such a stink?"

Harry looked out the window again. He couldn't imagine what she was talking about. "I'm sorry, Flora, you lost me. What thing?"

She pointed and said, "My birdfeeder—right there." The birdfeeder was about ten feet away, and a squirrel was sitting on it greedily spilling sunflower seeds. Until the day before, Harry hadn't even noticed the birdfeeder, even though he drove past it every day in his golf cart. Otherwise, it was only visible from Flora's kitchen.

"Charlie's sister gave it to me. Usually, I forget to fill it, but I'll be damned if I'll take it down now. I won't stand by and let that bitch Alice try to push her weight around. She thinks she's queen of the condos."

As it turned out, that damn birdfeeder had nearly caused his foursome to miss its tee time. When Harry dropped by to pick up his golf buddy Simon Morgan, his wife, Alice, had wrangled Harry into signing her petition to force the removal of Flora's birdhouse. "I signed the petition so you could keep it," said Harry, which was true because, later that same day, Martha Birnbaum had arrived with just such a petition. He gladly signed it and encouraged her to collect more signatures.

"You're a doll," said Flora.

Flora returned to the stove to perform more culinary theatrics, and Harry slipped over and stood close to her at the stove. Then he gently leaned against her, glancing down at her slimmed, solidified hips and waist, puzzled by what was different about them. She rattled the cover on the empty saucepan prop she had placed on the stove before she added a touch of pepper to the mysterious mixture and, finally, fiddled with the temperature controls, turning one up and then back down again.

Dinner went smoothly although, as she had feared, she never was able to pry Harry too far from the subject of his lazy twenty-five-year-old grandson. After dinner, Harry insisted on helping Flora clean up. "You spent hours in the kitchen," he said. "It's the least I could do."

She appreciated the gesture, but she was dying to release her confined body from its straight-jacket and snuggle onto the couch. Cleanup could wait until morning, and she was sick of Zeke, so she said she had a headache. Harry put his arm around her and held her close. "My fault," he said. "I talk too much." Ten minutes later, he left.

As soon as the door closed softly behind Harry, she slipped her dress off, unhooked all the stays, unzipped her girdle/corset/bustier, stepped out of it and, almost naked, feeling giddy and almost weightless, she danced a few steps around the room before flopping into Charlie's wing chair where her guest had sat. Harry wasn't perfect, but she had a warm feeling about him. Tomorrow she'd clean up the mess and go shopping for some equally powerful but more comfortable underwear.

Harry plodded home, sat in the dark for a few minutes, then turned the TV to a basketball game. He sighed, and although he had no interest in the game, there were too many thoughts in his head to sleep. He leaned back in the sofa and absentmindedly watched the flickering light from the TV dance around the room. He couldn't decide if Flora was superficial and silly or charming and genuine. But she seemed to understand him, knew how to please him, and knew how to make him comfortable.

The Mail

The mailboxes for 16, 17, and 18 Bristol Court were mounted on a single post along the curb on the widows' side of the street. At 11:30 the next morning, Harry walked across the street to check his mailbox. He saw Mildred emerge from her front door thirty seconds later with her coat wrapped around her shoulders, but he failed to notice the curtains stir in Flora's front window. Mildred approached the mailbox with her head down, watching her steps. Harry waited to greet her. "Hello, Mildred."

She looked up and smiled. "Oh, Harry, I'm frightfully sorry. I didn't see you."

Harry quickly sifted through his thin pile of mail and said, "Bills and junk. That's all I get."

Mildred, who didn't seem to have any mail at all, said, "Did you and Simon Morgan play eighteen yesterday?" Harry nodded. "So, he's back from his business trip."

"Got in late the night before. Barely made our tee time."

"That's nice," she said, smiling at him again as she brushed a wisp of hair from her face. "Well, have a nice day. I have to hurry—Monday lecture at the Prosser. I never miss it. So nice to see you, Harry."

"Yeah, it seems like we always meet at the mailbox." Harry, who gave no thought to Mildred's interest in Simon, ambled back across the street, set the mail on the hall table, went into the den, turned the television on, and flipped through the channels as he thought, *I've never been to a lecture in my life.*

After the art lecture, Mildred stopped at an antiques shop and then at an independent bookstore that served espresso superior to Starbuck's. Back home she gardened in her tiny backyard, prepared a light *crepes veronique,* dined alone, and cleaned up. Then she moved into her perfectly decorated and well-appointed living room and turned on the gas fireplace with the fake logs that burned but were never consumed. She read by the cone of light from the reading lamp next to her chair as darkness overtook the rest of the house.

What Flora Saw

Fretting about the birdfeeder meeting the next day, it was midnight when Flora turned out the lights and headed to her bedroom. As she glanced at her birdfeeder, out of the corner of her eye she thought she saw a silhouette in the dim security lights along the golf cart path. She watched as the figure of a man stepped carefully into Mildred's yard. But before she could grab the phone and dial 911, he stepped on something and hopped in pain. At the same instant, Mildred's back porch light flashed on and off, the door opened, Mildred's head appeared, and she more or less pulled the hopping intruder into her house.

Flora lay in bed, the worries about the birdfeeder replaced by a replay of the scene of Harry and Mildred chit-chatting at the mailbox. Could that shadowy figure have been Harry?

The Meeting

Harry arrived at Flora's in coat and tie in accordance with the club's dress code. Flora looked fabulous. He hadn't realized she had a waist. She usually looked lumpy. Last Sunday she had revealed a new shape, better but strange, firm and round, sort of like an ice cream cone. On this night she wore a red silk dress smoothly wrapped around her that displayed a real figure. She pirouetted for him.

"So, what do you think? I bought it at Nordstrom's today." He noticed her face was softer with less harsh color. "They helped me with the makeup, too. I think I had lost the hang of it."

"You look—you look wonderful." They set off in their finery in Flora's electric cart down the path along the third fairway.

The room was packed. Alice Morgan, who served on the condo board, was the instigator of the campaign to remove the birdfeeder. In accordance with Alice's interpretation of the rules, the Royce Management Company had told Flora to remove it, but Flora had appealed to the board. Harry and Flora ran into Simon at the door.

"I'm surprised to see you here, Simon," said Flora.

"Oh, I wouldn't miss this," said Simon. "I have a surprise for you, Harry." He handed Harry a golf ball. "That's your mark, isn't it?"

"Thanks," said Harry. "Where the hell did you find it?"

Simon laughed. "I stepped on it in the dark." Just then his wife rapped her gavel and called the meeting to order. Flora glanced at the ball as Harry slipped it into his jacket pocket. It was a Titleist.

Alice explained to the condo owners what they already knew; they could do as they liked to the interior of their homes, but the outside of the houses and all the grounds—landscaping included, even everyone's front and backyards—were maintained by a management company engaged by the condo association. Flora leaned toward Harry and said in a loud whisper, "That's interesting. What about Alice's flower garden?"

The anti-feeder speakers, of which there were many, seized on the concept of "precedent," and all said the same thing in slightly different ways: they had no problem with this particular birdfeeder which was tasteful and not unattractive, but it would set a precedent that, they implied, would soon lead to Bristol Court being overwhelmed by ugly birdfeeders.

Harry slouched in his chair and wondered how time could pass so slowly when a late arrival caught his attention. She made a stir, because there were hardly any vacant chairs, and several men rose to offer her a seat. Simon Morgan removed his jacket from the empty chair next to him, and the late arriving lady took the seat. Harry looked up and noticed that Alice Morgan, sitting at the head table, was glaring at the new arrival who had interrupted the meeting.

The new arrival turned toward Harry and smiled, but he had never seen her before. He'd thought by this time he had seen everyone on Bristol Court, especially the attractive women, of whom there were few. She was wearing a plain black dress, what Harry called a "cocktail dress". It was simple, with a round neck and long sleeves, but it clung to her slim figure in a fascinating way. Her lips had a hint of color. Her hair was silver and pulled up so it exposed her neck. Flora didn't seem to be paying her any attention, so Harry figured she must have known her.

Mona Finnigan pointed out that many birds had come to depend on the feeder and suggested they would starve if it were removed. Martha Birnbaum, the leader of the Flora supporters and a sweet lady, took even longer to point out the number of species who used the area as part of their migratory paths, several of which Harry had never heard of, including one called a tit, which struck him as amusing. Finally, someone shouted, "You forgot the blue-footed booby, Martha!" and Martha, a sweet old lady, turned and hissed through clenched teeth. "Who said that?"

Armond Zambini quoted from the United States Constitution and alleged that things had come to a sorry state when people had the right to carry a handgun and shoot each other but were forbidden to feed the poor, hungry birds. His booming voice and his speech were simultaneously ridiculous and moving.

Suddenly, the door to the meeting room flung open, and the condo association's attorney rushed to the front of the room in a flurry of paper. He apologized for being late, then announced that the motion under debate was out of order. The birdhouse was "explicitly" banned by the rules, which could be changed only by a two-thirds majority vote at the annual meeting, which would not take place for approximately eight months. The room erupted into mass confusion. Alice Morgan at the head table turned quietly to the chairman. He nodded, struck his gavel, and the board filed out of the room. The meeting was over. It was after six.

"Well, that's that," said Flora. "Let's go to dinner." As Flora and Harry stood, the beautiful stranger also stood and approached them. "Hello, Harry. Hello, Flora," she said.

"Hello, Mildred," said Flora.

Mildred, thought Harry, *another Mildred?* The woman gave Harry a strange look. "Don't you recognize me? Do I look that bad?"

It was Mildred—his neighbor Mildred. "I'm sorry," he stammered. "The dress. You changed your hair."

"Yes, it is quite a dress, isn't it?" said Flora. "Well, come along Harry."

Harry didn't budge. "I'm so sorry, Mildred. We're

staying at the club for dinner. Are you alone? Why don't you join us?"

Suddenly, Harry felt himself being yanked toward the door as Flora said, "I'm sure she has other plans."

Dinner At The Club

At the bar, Flora was greeted warmly by a few of her supporters. Her opponents avoided her and would not meet her eye unless Flora spoke to them, which she made a concerted effort to do.

Harry stopped in the men's locker room where all the talk was about Mildred.

In the Ladies Lounge, Flora ran into her chief supporter, Martha Birnbaum.

"So," said Martha, "what did you think of Mildred's dress?"

Flora looked around to see who was in earshot. "Alice better watch out," said Flora.

"Alice Morgan?"

"Trust me on this one, Martha," said Flora, raising her eyebrows knowingly.

They left the lounge together. "Uh, oh," said Martha, "here they come. See you later." Martha left hurriedly as Alice and Simon Morgan approached, arm in arm.

Flora moved behind a potted palm, then stepped out in front of them. "Well, hello, Alice," she said cheerfully.

"Flora," said Alice. "I'm so sorry about the last-minute lawyer thing. It took me totally by surprise, as you can imagine." She took Flora's hand. "I really, personally have no objection to the feeder, but I'm on the board, you know, and as a board member—"

"Oh, Alice," said Simon, "give it a rest."

"Actually, Alice," said Flora, "to tell you the truth I really don't give a shit one way or the other. By the way," she continued, "don't you think Mildred looked stunning tonight? She's finally coming out of her shell. It's been so hard for her since she lost Desmond." Alice and Simon exchanged a quick glance, but not quick enough for Flora to miss the look of dread on Alice's face. It was a moment Flora would cherish, worth a thousand bird feeders.

Flora drifted through the club dining room, bestowing a relaxed smile on friends and enemies alike, finally arriving at the corner table where Harry was waiting. He smiled. "You were gone so long I was beginning to worry about you," he said. He stood and held her chair for her. "I hope you're not too distressed about the way things went at the meeting, Flora."

Flora, unrestrained by her new undergarment, turned gracefully and bestowed a public and possessive kiss on Harry's cheek. "Harry," she said, "I don't think I've felt so wonderful in years. I'm so glad you got your four-dollar Titleist back." She then turned to the young man in the starched white jacket posted next to the table. "Thomas, Mr. Overmeyer will have a Canadian Club manhattan, and I shall have the same—with two cherries." She then turned to Harry, reached across the table, and squeezed his hand, the glow of triumph on her face.

CIRCUS CITY

UNTIL I found the box in the attic, my mother was a mystery to me.

She sells cars (a piece of information I hope my friends are unaware of), and I help her practice by being the customer. "I'm just looking," I say.

"Take your time, honey," she'll say. (Never push.)

I'll say, "You know, I'm not sure I'm ready to buy."

"Life is short," she'll say. (This is not pushing.)

"I'm a business person," I'll say. "Is a convertible a good investment?"

"If you want an investment, buy stocks. A car is a friend, a companion," she'll say. (That is redirection.)

My room is super neat because she insists that everything be put away and the bed made with tight corners as soon as I get up. She, Dad, and I eat all our meals together, and she makes us talk about what we're doing and what our friends are doing, and then we have to clean up, wash the dishes and put them away before we can be excused. I have lots of other dumb jobs like raking the leaves and dusting and taking out the trash. None of my friends' mothers make them do that stuff.

Sometimes Mom will just sit with a faraway look, and my father will say, "Let her be. She's at the circus," which I used to think was just his way of saying she was daydreaming. But then I found that box in the attic. There was a lot of stuff in it, but the best thing was a circus poster of a girl on a flying trapeze. In huge letters it read:

THE ASTOUNDING MARIA MANCINI
of the
FLYING MANCINIS

In the background, below the flying girl, was a circus ring filled with acrobats, clowns, dancing horses, jugglers, a ringmaster, and stands full of astounded people, all under a huge big top. The bottom of the poster read:

FLEMING CIRCUS – 26 ACTS –
COMING to GARRET CITY, IOWA –

JULY 21 and JULY 22 – TWO
SHOWS EACH DAY – PARADE
THURSDAY MORNING.

The poster was a little beat up—it had been folded twice—but it was so big and colorful that I thought it would look great on my bedroom wall, especially because my name is Maria, too. For some reason my mother was thrilled. "Sometimes your dad puts things away," she said, "and I can't find them." She insisted we go through the whole box together.

"Here's a new game," she said, looking at her watch. "Tell me when a minute is up. Count to yourself. Go!" I tried to count, but I lost track and finally said "Stop!" But Mom said that was only thirty-seven seconds, so I took her watch and said, "Go!" She picked up a pile of old postcards out of the box and thumbed through them, stood, left the room, returned, sat down, looked me in the eye, slapped the table, and said, "Stop!" It had been exactly one minute. "I practiced my moves on the trampoline every day," Mom said, gazing up at the poster, "but in the air, timing is more important. Timing is essential. George, Steve, and I had to practice counting one thousand one, one thousand two, one thousand three—like that. We'd chant together and count like a singing group, and then George would say, 'Okay, a hundred.' Then each of us would silently count and slap the table when we hit a hundred. We did that over and over until we all slapped the table at exactly the same instant. We had to be exact within a tenth of a second. The hard part is, when you're flying, time slows down and flows like water. When you let go of that trapeze bar you go up—you fly, you are weightless. You feel the air, smell it, see it—the shafts of spotlight piercing the smoke and hitting you—the smell of the circus. I was above it all, alone, a little girl, flying."

I stared at my mother who was wearing her familiar, faraway expression, and then I glanced at the poster and back at her again. "Are you saying…?"

"Now you know why we named you Maria," she said. "And you thought I was just the best car saleswoman in Park City. Isn't life full of surprises?"

"What are you talking about? *Your* name isn't Maria. And who's George? Who's Steve?"

"Well, let's see. I was in an act with two men, George and Steve. We were called the Flying Mancinis. George was called Georgio, and Steve was Francesco. I was Maria. They were supposed to be brothers, and I was billed as their niece. That's what the posters said. George was the catcher."

"The catcher? What kind of act has a catcher?"

"A trapeze act. For four years I was the star of the circus, skinny little Sally Jones from the middle of Florida. I learned it all from George. My parents were jugglers. I had been one of the Little Tumblers. I could do cartwheels and flips better than anyone. But when George's wife became pregnant, they chose me to become a Flying Mancini. I did it for four years. George made us practice at least four hours a day. Together, we checked every piece of equipment before every practice and before every performance, tied every knot, put up every swing, and tested each one. The most important thing is to know how to fall. Everybody falls. You have to learn to fall exactly the right way. You have to relax when you fall, not tense up, and you have to trust the net.

"We practiced our moves on the trampoline every day, but timing is more important. Timing is essential. Like I said, we had to be exactly on time every time, within a tenth of a second. Think about a tenth of a second. How long is that? That's how long we had to make a catch work. Even that tenth of a second gets broken down into smaller fractions. When you first feel the hair on the arm of the catcher with your fingertips, that's when the tenth of a second starts. Then for the rest of that tenth of a second, as you close your hand one finger at a time, you adjust your grip. At the same time, you feel his hand wrap around your arm as you each squeeze tighter and tighter. It has to be perfect, or you fall. You have to do all that in midair, in a tenth of a second. As you're doing it, as you focus on all the steps, it seems much longer, but that's all it is: a tenth of a second.

"One night in Covington, Kentucky, on the Ohio River across from Cincinnati, people from Ringling Brothers came and watched me. They'd heard about the skinny little girl. They said I was something special. They wanted me. I talked about it with my parents and with George and Steve and everybody. I wasn't sure. The Ringling people said I should think about it. Each of the next two winters, Ringling called my dad in Florida and asked if I was still thinking about it.

"Then, my last season, when I was not skinny

anymore, Steve told my parents he wanted to marry me. I was sixteen; Steve was thirty. My dad said absolutely not. Steve was okay with that. Maybe he expected it. I don't know. He was an easygoing guy. There was a performance that same night, and Steve and I said we'd do it. Dad said okay; we were professionals. George refused. He was angry. He called Steve a fool and said he'd ruined everything. He and Steve went on alone that night. Steve decided to try a double. I thought sure George would drop him on purpose. When they did the double, it was close. It all took less than a second. Steve was a little off. George was supposed to hang from his knees on the bar, but he realized Steve was late, so when Steve was in midair performing his double somersault, George slipped down so that only his ankles and toes were on the bar. He caught Steve with just his hands in the last little bit of that tenth of a second. I still remember the gasp of the crowd. Every paying customer and every performer was nervous the rest of the night. Even the dog act were off. The dogs knew.

"That was the end of it; that night Steve proposed. I never performed again.

"My parents asked me if I wanted to go to Ringling Brothers. Ringling would take me without George or Steve. It would be a lot of money, and I'd be a star. I said what I really wanted was to be an ordinary girl and go to high school. That November I enrolled full time in Park City High School. My parents found the little house here and my aunt came and stayed with me while the circus traveled. I spent almost two full school years right here at Park City High School. I was way behind at first, but I ended up on the honor roll."

When I went to bed that night, I continued looking through the box. I found letters from Mom's parents, a couple from Ringling Brothers, but no letters from Steve. There were six postcards, the ones she had picked out of the box earlier, from places I had never heard of in six different states. They were addressed to her and signed "Steve," but there were no messages on any of them.

The next day Mom said she was taking me to Circus City. We drove through downtown, past the warehouses, across the tracks, and stopped next to a big, empty lot. "How much further?" I said. She smiled. We got out of the car and sat together on a park bench covered with graffiti that looked out on an almost flat expanse of dirt and clumps of crabgrass, about ten treeless acres. "Welcome to Circus City," she said.

"Mom, this is nothing. It's just dirt."

"No, Maria, right here is a little city. We parked our trailer here from November through February every year. This is the only place I can call home, although I was here only four months a year. You can still see it on old road maps dating back to the 1940s and 50s. After that, Park City grew around Circus City, and the name "Circus City" disappeared from the maps.

"Our caravan traveled from March to October, from small town to county fairgrounds, Florida to Texas, then up to the border of Canada, but never into Canada itself.

By July we'd be heading east to New England until Labor Day, then we'd slowly make our way back here to Circus City by November. At each stop we'd raise our huge tent in the dark of night and turn an empty field into a land of magic and fantasy. Then, after a few days, following the last show, in only a few hours, again in the dark, we would turn the magic and the fantasy back into an empty, well-trodden, muddy field once more. Before dawn we were back on the road. We didn't follow the railroad like the big circuses. We followed the highways, mostly the blue ones.

"The Fleming Circus is gone now. It folded a couple years after I left. It happened all over the country. It used to be that a circus would come to almost every town. There were a few famous three-ring circuses and countless smaller ones, like ours, that toured rural towns. Even though we could draw crowds wherever we went, it was only for a few days—a week at most. It was how we existed. We were nomads. Everybody in my circus is gone, scattered around the globe—some returned to eastern Europe, some to Asia, Europe, the Americas—wherever home was for them."

I gazed around the empty lot, trying to picture it full of trailers and tents and animals and people and trampolines. I couldn't, but I glanced at my mother, and I knew she could.

"Every family had a trailer, and all the trailers traveled all over the country together. The trailers were our little houses. I even had my own tiny room. It was this big," she said, spreading her arms and making a pirouette. "Everything I owned was in that room, stored in a nook or cranny, under my bed, above my head, inside a footstool. If you took one thing out, you had to put it back before you got the next thing out.

"The big top was put up over there, and that was where we ate, every meal, all of us together, everybody—the artists, the clowns, the trainers, the musicians."

"Did you have midgets?"

"We did, but they were just ordinary people to me. The circus was real. We were all together in a hot, huge tent full of animals and canvas and popcorn and cigars and cotton candy and straw and hay and mud and sweat—real smells—not air fresheners or dryer sheets."

"Tell me more about Steve."

"I still think about him," Mom said, staring across the crabgrass as if she could see him standing there. "I could always tell what Steve was thinking, and I knew he knew what I was thinking. One thing we did was that George would catch Steve, and then Steve would catch me. George's catch was sure and strong, like he doubted me a little and had to do it all himself. But Steve's catch was gentle, more trusting. He knew I was strong, and I would do my part. I know I'll never be that close to anyone again. I'm not sure I want to be. I didn't love him. But he was the daring young man on the flying trapeze, and he was nice to me."

"What did you two talk about?"

"About the act. About our timing, our moves."

"That's all?"

"Pretty much," she said. "Steve wasn't a big talker. He didn't even tell me he wanted to marry me. He just asked my dad. That's how I found out."

The next morning, Mom was gone. Dad told me not to worry. He took the poster down, put it back in the box, and put the box back in the attic. "Let's go get her," he said. In the car he said, "Opening that box was not a good idea. Your mother came from another planet, a whole other world of people she loved and, except for Gramma and Grampa Jones, people she will never see or hear from again. She was torn from them one day when she was only sixteen. To you and me the circus is magical—to her, it's real."

There she was, in Circus City, sitting on the bench again. Dad sat on one side of her, and I sat on the other. "I put the box back in the attic," he said. "Shall we leave it there for a while?"

"Okay," said Mom as she stared wistfully across the field of dirt.

"Mom," I said, "you told me yesterday you could tell what Steve was thinking." She turned and fastened her eyes on me. "So how come you didn't know he wanted to marry you?"

She returned to her distant gaze, blinked, and said, "Well, maybe not everything." Then she cocked her head as if she had experienced an epiphany and said, "It's funny how, when you talk about somebody, you realize things about them you hadn't realized before, like there was a drawer in your brain you'd forgotten about. And inside that drawer was a slip of paper that said, 'You really didn't know Steve, did you?'" Then she gave Dad and me each a big hug and said, "Let's go home."

On the way she said, "I got over Steve pretty quick. I had a high school boyfriend. We went to the prom together. He gave me a corsage and rented a limo. We talked about chemistry. I loved his brain. He taught me that all the elements that make up everything, from hydrogen to uranium, were created in the first few seconds of the universe and, if you compress the billions of years since then into one year, all recorded history would only be the last ten seconds, so I suppose my time in the circus was a lot less than a tenth of a second. He didn't propose to me. He didn't even try to kiss me. It was an ordinary and mysterious and wonderful high school relationship."

"The perfect man," I said.

"Not exactly. I wanted him to kiss me."

"So when did you meet Dad?"

"I just told you—in high school."

"But you said he didn't ask you to marry him."

"He didn't. I asked him."

We still play the car-selling game where I pretend to be a customer, but I never pretend I'm from the circus. So far, Mom's other life has stayed in the attic, but sometimes I do catch her with that faraway look, and I know she's visiting another planet.

THE BULL

J. C.

I raise cattle, beef cattle, right here on this ranch, and I have one bull; he weighs about 4,000 pounds, and they say he looks fearsome, but he ain't. Mostly, he just stands out in the field like a piece of furniture.

I have a lot of the cows artificially inseminated, but the bull handles as many as he can, because for me, and the bull, and probably even the cows, the natural way is better. I'm thinking of trading the bull for another one to improve the bloodline, if you know what I mean.

The other day I ran into my ex-wife at Garrett's Department Store. I was in the city to buy a lamp for the living room. I wanted to spruce up the place. Don't know what she was doing in the furniture department, except I know she likes furniture. Always did. I ended up buying a lot of stuff: end tables, even a leather sofa. She helped. She's a good shopper. Then we went out for a cup of coffee.

"How are the boys?" she asked. I just kind of looked at her. "Listen, J.C., I write to them, and I call them, but they don't call back, and they never write. I try."

"I'll speak to them."

We got two sons, and they've done real well. Went to college. Albert, he lives over in Fairmont. Married. Got his own farm and a kid on the way. Jimmy, he lives up on Long Island. That's in New York. He took me to a party up there once. They had this thing called "valet parking." I hope I said that right. You drive up and this kid takes your car and drives away. Then when you're ready to go, another kid brings it back. It's the damnedest thing.

I used to be married, but it didn't work out. I'm not saying anything about her, but I had custody of the kids.

"You did a good job, J.C.," the ex said after I brought her up to date on the kids. I raised 'em pretty good. I'm proud of that.

"I wish one of them had become a soldier," I said. "We owe our country that, but they went their own way."

"You got two perfect sons, smart enough not to want to get themselves killed," she said, "and you're not happy." She ran her hand through her hair, which was the look she had when she came out of the shower, but now she had some kind of fancy hairdo. "So, you're finally fixing the place up. Today you spent over a thousand dollars on stuff you never let me spend a nickel on." She shook her head. Of course, we didn't have the money back then, but I didn't say nothin'.

She asked me how many cattle I was up to and how many miles of barbed wire I had run. I told her there were about four hundred head now and almost three miles of fence, which takes a lot of time. "Got the combine ready for harvest," I said. "I'm thinking about adding some silage to the hay. Did some deworming last week and castrated six calves, two more than same time last year."

"Uh-huh. That's great, J.C. And then, in the evening, you go into your office and write it all down and check it twice." She understood that, on a cattle ranch, keeping and maintaining detailed records is essential. "You still doing it all on your own?" I nodded. I live alone. My brother Billy lives down the road a mile. I keep a neat house, and Billy likes it messy. That's why he moved out. No hard feelings. Billy comes over and helps when I need him, but he works at the cement factory until five, so it has to be before or after that. "You let the dogs in the house yet?"

"Of course not." She was wearing something like a man's suit tailored for a woman. She must be some kind of professional these days, but I didn't ask.

She said she had just played in a bridge tournament. I asked what that was, and she said, "You know what bridge is, J.C. Remember, I tried to teach you, and you paid attention for about one minute." I didn't remember that at all. "Let me see your hands," she said. "Your hands were so rough and strong." She took my hands in hers. "So rough," she said. Her hand was timid. I always had to think about being gentle so as not to hurt her.

When she stood up from the table to leave, she said, "It was good to see you, J.C." Then she smiled. "You seein' anybody?"

"Nope," I said, "just me, livin' alone, the way I like it," which wasn't exactly true.

"That's good," she said. "There's a lot of lucky women in the world. By that I mean all the women who haven't fallen for that look in your eye." Then she kissed me and said, "I'll always love you, J.C., but you'll always be impossible."

The furniture got delivered, and I just put all the old stuff in a pile out by the road. The neighbors would take it. The new furniture made the rest of the house look terrible, so I covered all the new stuff with old sheets and started scraping and painting.

Maude

I live in the house I grew up in. It's a big old white farm-house—used to be a farm around it, barns and everything. Now just the house is left, and most all the furniture, of course, the most dramatic piece of which is the feather sofa. It's huge—big and brown mostly and kind of tweedy, but soft because it has feathers in the cushions. Some are sticking out—little feathers—goose feathers—"down." It's kind of lumpy, but since the lumps are filled with down, it's comfortable, even if you sit on a lump. Mamma died on that sofa under the crazy quilt that her mamma's mamma had made. We threw the quilt out, but I kept the sofa.

My brother Norbert lived in the house a long time after Mamma died. Then my boyfriend, Morris, moved in, and then it was the three of us. And that was fine. There's plenty of room. Morris and Norbert, they hardly talked to each other, but they talked to me, and that worked out. It wasn't great, but it worked.

Morris is a big man—lazy—lazy in a good way—strong and lazy. And Morris loved the sofa. That's where Morris was. Made some permanent dents in the sofa. And I got the habit of waiting on him. But then I realized that wasn't good for him, so I stopped waitin' on him. "Get it yourself," I'd say. But…no, I don't mean *but,* I mean to say although…no, I don't mean that either. So, anyway, Morris left, and then Norbert finally got a job, and he moved out. Said he missed Morris, which I never believed for a minute.

So I've been alone for a year now. Well, once in a while Aunt Doris comes and stays overnight. She sleeps on the sofa, although there's three empty bedrooms. "Where's that old quilt?" she always asks. We talk like a house afire, but she never stays more than one night, then she goes back to Topeka and rambles around her empty house. I never visit her. She talks way too much.

I miss Morris. He was a good listener. Never said it was a bad day. Actually, I don't miss him so much lately because I met this guy. We go out for a drink sometimes;

that is, I meet him at Jimmy's a couple nights a week. His name is J.C. Actually, his real name is James but, as he says, "They call me J.C."

He doesn't talk so much but, well, I like to dance. He likes it too. I can tell by the way he moves, the way his face relaxes.

Billy

My brother J.C. is a clean, hardworking man. Raised two kids up right after his wife walked out on him. She was in the wrong but, well, in some ways I don't blame her, and I didn't feel that way until I tried living with J.C. Life is hard for him. Not that it needs to be. It just is. He's not mean or nasty about it, but what it boils down to is everything is his way or no way. Everything.

Like when I moved out, J.C. took on the phone company, which nobody that's not crazy ever does. He got all wound up in a snarl because, as J.C. tells the story, when I moved out, they wanted to charge him for a phone and me for a phone. His idea, which he told the phone company, was to just keep the same number for both of us, and we'd split the cost, but they wouldn't do it. So he ran a line across the fields to my house, almost a mile, and now the phone rings at both houses. It's not real handy because, well, if I'm here I'll always answer and likewise for J.C. If not, well, people just got to call back—unless I'm at J.C.'s or he's over here, which is sometimes, but not very much. Another problem is, we can't call each other.

I went over to live with my brother after his boys both left because, us both being alone, it seemed the natural thing to do. Now, although I moved out, I got to go over to J.C.'s almost every night, tryin' to unconfuse him because he's met this woman, and the two of them together is somethin' to watch.

Her brother is Norbert Peabody, who is an easygoin' guy. He told me about this guy named Morris that used to live with them—a big, fat guy who just sat around all day but, somehow, Maude really liked him, and Norbert says that after Morris left, she sat around staring at the sofa like Morris was still sitting there doin' nothin', so Norbert left, and now she lives alone, and she meets J.C., and that changed everything, and I say watch out. I never had a girlfriend or anything close to that, but I know there's good things about having a woman, like a romance, I mean, but there's also other things, complications and such, and I know Norbert agrees with me on that. It's just askin' for trouble.

J. C. and Maude—they're both lonely, which I suppose is their own fault, but there it is. I like her. You can't help but like her. She soft-talked me into spending one weekend at J.C.'s so they could take this bus trip to the Zydeco Festival, and they came back all stuck on each other.

So he asked her to move in with him, and she said yes. They were even talkin' about marriage.

One night me and J.C. was over to her house, and she was talking about what she was gonna bring when she moved in. Some realtor had just left. She has a house full of furniture, and you know women and furniture. So she started naming what she might bring, like this chair or that table, and he kept shaking his head, and finally she mentions the sofa, and he says, "Please, Maude, not the sofa. I got a perfectly good sofa. I don't care what you else you bring to clutter up the house, but I ain't havin' them loose chicken feathers flyin' all over."

She started to cry, and that surprised both of us. I never seen her cry before. Then she left the room and left J.C. and me sitting on that sofa, sipping our beers.

In about five minutes she came back into the room, carrying a shotgun. "Get up," she said, and we scrambled as she fired about ten rounds of buckshot into that sofa, and they was feathers all over the place.

"There," she said, "now get out, the both of you," and me and J.C. left.

J.C.

I didn't see her for a long time. She plain stopped coming to Jimmy's. All I was seein' was Billy, and I was getting' damn sick of him.

Then one night she just showed up all smiles and talking to me like it was the day before she blasted that sofa with her shotgun and told me to get out, like it never even happened.

So we started up again and, as it turned out, the Zydeco Festival was comin' up again. We're sitting on the grass listenin' to the music, far enough away from the stage so we can talk. "So," she said, "I know it's about a year old but, I was wondering, is that offer to move in with you, is that still open?"

I didn't say anything for a minute, and then I said, "I don't know," which was the truth.

"Okay, well, anyway, what I really need to know is this: Let's just say that it was still open, and let's say I got a chair instead of that sofa—the one you couldn't live with. Let's just say that. I mean, I'm not saying I got one or would want to bring it if I did. But let's say I did get a chair, and it had feathers, and I said I wanted to accept your offer to move in, which I understand might not still be open, but let's say it was." She sat back and looked at me. I didn't say anything. "Well?" she said.

"Oh, boy," I said. "So, this is purely theoretical like."

"Totally hypothetical."

"What's that?"

"Same thing. You can think about it. Take your time. Now, let's dance."

The Bull

The week after the Zydeco Festival, J.C. went to auction. He looked everything over but didn't bid once. So that old bull is still there. Most of the day he stands stock still. He prefers the middle of his field. Sometimes snow will sit on his back, and there are no tracks around him, so you know he has not moved for hours. When he is still, his muscles seem to ripple. There might be a switch of his tail. He watches the cows grazing in the field beyond the fence. With equal interest he may turn his head and study the old red bicycle with the bent frame that leans against the barn. For only a year he gamboled and ran and jumped, and then he became strong and solid and gentle and slow. His memories are of that first year and that he mated with about half the cows over the past three years. And his meals, the same each day. He eats only what he needs. He's content most of the day to stand and stare. Sometimes he lies down, but most of the time he stands stock still in the center of his field. He sees what he sees and knows what he knows.

EDITH'S SUMMER

EDITH spent most of her day talking to a cow she had named Albert. Three days after summer vacation started, she wandered along Spring Creek, being careful where she stepped, as Albert moseyed along beside her. "This summer will never, ever end," said Edith. Albert's sad eyes seemed to understand.

"Why do you spend so much time with that cow?" asked her mother.

Edith shrugged.

"Find something else to do, Edith."

In the morning, as the air filled with the sounds of the birds and the farm animals starting their days, Edith was silent. She sat on a stool on the back porch, her forehead resting on the railing, her hands drooping at her side, a picture of despair. Next to Edith, her grandmother was sorting green beans, snapping the ends off the good ones. Even though her hands were gnarled up like fists, she was good at the bean job. "You look busy," she said to Edith.

"I'm not," said Edith. Then she looked up and sighed a grown-up sigh, a sigh out of all proportion to her small stature. "Grandma, do *you* think it's a bad thing that I talk to Albert?"

Grandma said she thought it was good for Albert, and it probably wasn't doing Edith any harm, but that, whatever the case, Edith should try to find something else to do, at least until her mother forgot about Albert, which wouldn't take long.

"But Grandma, there is absolutely nothing to do. It's so boring around here. There's nobody to play with. Mother and Father work all the time. Being eight is hard."

"Try being eighty," said Grandma. "You want to play cards?"

"What game?"

"You choose."

"I only know one."

Mother thought that was a good idea. Since there was nothing else to do, Edith said okay. Grandma loved to play cards. At first, Edith won almost every game, and she liked to win, then Grandma started winning, and they discovered Edith did not like to lose.

Edith and Grandma wasted beautiful sunny summer afternoons sitting at the kitchen table where Edith's mother was trying to cook or iron or sew. Edith and Grandma played cards every day and got into huge fights. *How can you get into fights playing Go Fish?* Edith's mother wondered.

"Do you have any threes?"

"Go fish."

"Yes, you do. I just saw you pick one up."

"That's cheating."

"I wasn't trying to look, so it's not cheating."

"Yes, it is."

Mother took the cards away. For a few days Grandma and Edith simmered. They did not speak a single word to each other.

Finally, Mother kicked them both out of the house. "Go talk to Albert," she said.

Edith and Grandma took a walk in the meadow and sat down on the bank of Spring Creek among the grazing cows. They pulled the tall grasses, bit the sweet juice from the tip, lay back, and gazed at the clouds. Albert, as usual, was grazing close by, close enough so Edith could hear him biting and chewing the sweet grass himself. When they were in the meadow, the three of them were always close together.

"What are we going to do about Mother?" asked Edith. "She's driving me crazy."

"I have no idea," said Grandma. "She hid the cards and won't tell me where they are."

"You're her mother, aren't you? You can tell her what to do. Tell her to leave me alone."

"Sorry. I tried. I did everything I could. But after

she turned two, she stopped listening to me and started doing just what she wanted."

"Well, tell me what I should do," said Edith. "This can't go on."

"I think the best thing is just let her go her own way."

"She wants to dress me and make me do chores and read books and stuff. I mean, I can just barely read. One book would take forever. This morning she said I had to learn how to cook. Can you imagine? I'm only eight."

"Yes, well, she does the same thing to me. She keeps bringing home dresses she wants me to wear. Potato sacks with flowers painted on them. I hate flowers. I just ignore her."

"Sheesh," said Edith, "it's hopeless."

After a few minutes, Grandma said, "It wouldn't kill you to learn how to cook."

"Forget it, Grandma."

Lying in the grass beside the lazy creek, watching the clouds drift and reshape themselves, Grandma turned toward Edith and said, "You know, Edith, your Albert is a girl."

"We've been over this before, Grandma. Albert is a boy. You're just trying to start an argument."

Grandma took the weed from her mouth and tickled Edith's nose. "Edith, all of the cows are girls. They give milk. Only females give milk. The bulls are boys; the cows are girls."

Not in the mood for Grandma's silliness, Edith brushed the weed away and rubbed her nose. "Grandma,

I have known Albert since he was a calf. I really do not care to discuss it further. He is a boy."

"All right, Edith—if you say so." Grandma patted Edith's arm. "I used to think that horses were boys and cows were girls, but I learned that I was wrong, and now I see that I am apparently wrong again." Then she drifted off into one of her naps.

Edith stood and looked down at her eighty-year-old grandma lying in the grass with a weed between her lips, her interlaced fingers crossed over her chest, which was slowly rising and falling with each breath. Edith wandered over to Albert. When she was close to him, he made soft little noises that meant something. She knew he had been listening when Grandma called him a girl. "Can you believe all that nonsense?" she whispered into his ear.

Grandma and Edith visited the pasture and sat by the creek every day, and that made Edith's mother happy but, now that the cards were hidden and the issue of whether Albert was a boy was settled, there wasn't much to argue about, so they just studied the sky.

Edith didn't do her chores, and her dad didn't push her. He was spoiling her, her mother said, and he agreed. Grandma never mentioned the chores one way or another.

Edith walked over to the apple tree next to the stream. Grandma's eyes were looking up. She patted the grass.

Edith lay down next to her and looked up too. Overhead, a hawk was circling. Crows were cawing in the apple tree. "What are they talking about?" asked Grandma.

"Who?" said Edith. "I don't hear anybody."

"The crows. They're cawing. What are they cawing about?"

"I have no idea."

"Well, you and Albert talk. You understand Albert. Why can't you understand the crows?"

"Because they are talking to each other. Albert talks to me."

"I see," said Grandma, feeling around for a new stalk of grass without taking her eyes off the hawk.

"Really, Grandma, I can understand Albert. Honest."

"I see."

Edith watched the hawk, wings spread, making perfect circles.

"But," said Edith, "fish don't talk. They just swim around. I watch them. They swim right past each other. They don't even look at each other. They couldn't hear each other anyway, not underwater. They don't have brains. If they did, they wouldn't get caught."

"Is that your final word on the subject?" asked Grandma.

"Yes. And squirrels communicate with their tails and tell each other where the nuts are, and bees buzz, and—"

"Oh, be quiet," said Grandma. "You're jabbering like a squirrel yourself. Just listen. Lay still. Open your ears. Close your eyes."

Edith listened to the sounds of the meadow. When she sat still and opened her ears, she could hear the birds and the animals talking to each other. Then she opened her eyes and noticed that rabbits didn't talk, but cows touched each other.

The next day under the apple tree, Edith said, "Here's what I think. You may be right that Albert doesn't actually talk, but I *can* understand him, not so much his words but, I mean, I understand him. I really do. Honest. The noises he makes are part of it, but they may not be actual words. So what I think is that animals talk without words. They do it mostly with touching—with their tails or paws or wings or whatever they have—and the noises are not really words."

"But not fish," said Grandma.

"No, not fish. I'm sure about that."

Grandma peered at the sky and smiled to herself. "Well, well, well," she said. "If animals can communicate that way, without words, then how come you and I can't? Aren't we smarter than a cow? I know I am. But maybe you aren't."

"Don't be silly. Of course I am. If you could do it, I could do it."

"Harrumph," snorted Grandma.

Edith jumped up onto her knees and leaned over her grandma as she said, "Of course we could do it too, you and me. This is the best idea you ever had. No talking. I bet we can do it."

"I'm not so sure your mother will approve."

Edith's face was an inch from her grandmother's nose. "Who cares?" Grandma was smiling and shaking her head. "What's the matter, Grandma? Are you chicken?"

"You mean I won't have to listen to all your nonsense anymore?"

"And I won't have to listen to yours either, except you still get to read me a story every night."

"What if I fall in a hole? Can I holler for help?"

"No, you have to moo like Albert would if he fell in a hole."

"I still don't think you can do it," said Grandma.

"Well, we'll see about that."

So they tried it for a week. Edith and Grandma communicated with each other like the animals. They stayed close together all day and communicated but did not talk, being silent pretty much all the time, unless they were way out in the meadow and Mother and Father were nowhere in sight.

It worked fine most of the time, but not so well in the kitchen or at the dinner table. Mother just didn't seem to be able to do it. She barely even tried. At the dinner table they would point and nod. Father just laughed, and he would pass the candlestick or say, "Are you trying to tell me you want some ketchup on your head?" Mother just sat there with her lips tight.

During the second week they were still doing great, at least Grandma and Edith thought so until Edith gestured for the milk pitcher and knocked Mother's water glass over. Mother calmly picked it up and said, "I think I've had enough of this grunting and flapping."

"Mother," said Edith, "we are just doing what Father does every day. He knows when the cows are hungry, when they need to be milked, which ones need settling down, and he works hard to make them comfortable, but he couldn't do any of that unless he and the cows were communicating without talking."

"It was bad enough," said Mother, "when you and your Grandma talked nonsense to each other all day long, but this is worse. Now it's got to stop, at least at the dinner table."

The August days were lazy and hot, and Grandma and Edith spent more and more time in the meadow. Then one aimless afternoon something dreadful happened. They saw a fox catch and kill a mouse right in front of their eyes, just across the creek. But the fox didn't kill the mouse right away. He played with it. He tortured it.

Now that Edith knew the mice communicated with each other and that they had families, she did not like the fox's behavior at all. She watched the fox take the live mouse by one little leg and shake it like a rag. The leg fell off, and the rest of the mouse went flying as it yelped in agony. And that was not the end of it. The mouse kept struggling helplessly. Edith stared in horror. Then she shook. Then she sobbed. "Why?" she sobbed, "why is the fox doing that? Why, Grandma, why?"

"There is no why," said Grandma, not knowing exactly how to respond. "He just is."

Edith reclined next to Grandma, and they rested there in the grass. There was nothing left to say.

Edith sobbed and sobbed. She sobbed in her mother's arms and in her father's lap. It was the fox's nature, they said. It was how the fox survived. Hunters kill deer. Farmers kill animals. That's where meat comes from—chickens, turkeys, and cows.

"Cows?" said Edith.

One morning Grandma did not get up. She stayed in bed and Mother called Dr. Petrie, who arrived right away.

Grandma had been sick for three days. Mother was in the kitchen preparing a tray for her. Edith noticed there was more on the tray than tea; there also was soup and bread. "Can I go with you to see her?"

"Maybe tomorrow," said Mother, who looked tired.

"Tell her I saw a hawk today."

"Why don't you draw her a picture?" Edith slid her picture under the door of Grandma's bedroom. Finally, after two more days, she was allowed to see her grandma, who was sitting up in bed and looking the same as always. "Why didn't you let me see you?"

"I was sick."

"You don't look sick. I saw a hawk in the meadow." Grandma raised her eyebrows. "That was the picture I drew. It was a picture of the hawk."

Grandma took the picture from her nightstand, held

it up, studied it, and hoped she had it right side up. She had thought it was a rocket crashing toward the Earth. "Tell me about it."

"Well," said Edith, "it was circling. Going around and around in the sky—you know, like you and me saw—and then he stopped and dropped, like he changed from a bird to a pointed bullet. That's what I drew. Those lines are speed lines. He is going faster and faster, and his feet are stuck out like this. They were big. This is his feet I drew here, maybe not quite this big. Down here. This is the bunny." Edith stopped talking.

Now Grandma understood the mystery of the bunny ears in the bottom corner of the picture. She did not ask what happened. They eyed each other. "It was sad what happened to the bunny," said Edith.

"But it must have been exciting."

Edith's eyes grew bigger. She nodded. She knew Grandma would understand. "You should have seen it," said Edith. "That's why I drew the picture. I didn't tell Albert about it or Mother. It would be hard for them to understand. Do you want to play cards? Do you want to go out in the meadow?"

"Maybe in a few days."

Finally, Mother said Grandma might be able to get out of bed if Edith would make dinner, and so she did. Everyone pronounced it delicious, although Edith noticed there was a lot left over.

They played cards, and Edith lost. Then they ventured

into the meadow and lay on a blanket under the stars. "Just for a few minutes," Mother said. The Milky Way spread across the sky. They lay close together so they could feel each other's warmth.

"Next week I'll be in third grade," said Edith.

"Good riddance is what I say. You made me waste my whole summer."

"Will you miss me?"

"Not for a second. Albert and I will sit under the apple tree and talk every day," said Grandma. "Do you think I could teach him to play cards?"

"Careful, Grandma, he might beat you."

"I wouldn't care if he did."

"Liar."

"I'd let him beat me the way I let you beat me."

"Liar. You never, ever did that."

"Well, I tried, but you weren't smart enough."

"Very funny," said Edith. It was so quiet, and the stars were so bright.

"Look, Edith, a shooting star. Make a wish."

Edith saw it. She could have wished the summer would never end, but she didn't. "My meatloaf didn't come out so good, did it?"

"To tell the truth, it tasted like cat food."

"Yup, it did. Mother probably won't ask me to cook dinner again for a while."

"God, I hope not," said Grandma, and she closed her eyes.

FAMILY

"BEFORE you go, a word." This was one of Dr. Miller's irritating expressions. He led Matilda to a bench in a private garden of the hospice and said, "June is fading. It might be any day." Her little sister would die—maybe before the weekend.

June's daughter still had not arrived. Matilda returned to June's room and sat next to the bed.

"I thought you were leaving," said June.

"I am, but I had a chat with the doctor," said Matilda.

"You mean, *a word,*" said June. "What was it?"

"Nothing much, just some financial stuff I already knew," lied Matilda. "June, I thought you said Beth would be here today." The doctor had gone on to say he was increasing June's pain meds to keep her comfortable. The cancer had spread beyond control. "I'd better call her now," said Matilda.

"Stop worrying. She'll be here. It's not like I'm going anywhere. Beth is busy," said June. "I've been trying to remember stuff. When did Mom and Dad die?"

"Thirty-five years ago next month, April 20," Matilda said.

"You have a great memory."

"You were only ten."

Matilda remembered all of it.

She had been on the way to her locker, taking her time, a new white kerchief tied around her neck, wondering when Bobby Townsend would show up. She had opened her locker and peered into the little mirror secured only by a paper clip. She'd have to wipe off the makeup before she went home (her mother was strict about makeup), and they'd probably make Matilda stay home with the brat while they went out for dinner. As she looked in the mirror, there was a tap on her shoulder. It was Bobby.

"Hey," he said, "how ya doin'?"

She turned and flashed a pink smile. "Hey, Bobby."

"Whatcha doin' Saturday?"

"None of your business."

"See ya around."

She'd stuffed her books into her locker, then touched the shoulder he had touched. Bobby was a senior. There was another tap on her shoulder. She swung around to face Mr. Marshall, the principal. He escorted her to his office. There had been an automobile accident—a bad one.

An hour later she sat in the emergency room, still in her bobby sox, white scarf, poodle skirt, and makeup, which she didn't need to worry about anymore. June, the spoiled brat, was with her and kept begging for nickels for the machine. "Are Mommy and Daddy going to be all right?" asked June. "Can we go home now?"

By morning they were home, alone together, Matilda and June. Their parents were gone.

Somehow, Matilda got herself through high school. What happened to Bobby? Who knows? He never tapped her shoulder again. He disappeared, more or less, a sort of ghost she passed now and then in the school hallways.

She'd saved the house, barely. There was insurance money, some government assistance, some part-time work—enough to survive and get June through school—even college. Matilda found a job at the Morrisdale Public Library and, under at the tutelage and kindness of the librarian, Ethel Kitters, eventually took over pretty much the whole job of running the library.

She also remembered the night she came home from the library, five years later, almost to the day, and entered their parent's bedroom, which she had kept meticulously clean. She opened the closet door and the clothes were gone. She screamed.

"It's been years, Matilda," said June. "I took it all to Goodwill."

"All of it? You should have asked."

"You'd have said no. It's time. I'm moving in here, unless you want to, which I know you don't." That night

Matilda hated June, hated her baby sister who had ruined her life just by existing.

As June drifted off to sleep, Matilda ventured into the garden and called Beth. "Aunt Tilly, I'm so glad you're with Mom. I'm trying to get away. I'll be there in a couple days."

"Beth, listen. I called because I just talked to the doctor. He thinks your mother will die this week—any day, he said. You have to get here tomorrow."

"Oh, dear. All right, I understand. I'll be there. I better make some phone calls. Can't wait to see you, Aunt Tilly." She hung up. Beth had always been a day late and a dollar short.

Next morning, Matilda drove back to the hospice. If Beth wasn't there, she'd call her again. June was asleep, and there was a pregnant young woman in the lobby. Matilda took her phone out of her purse to call Beth. The young pregnant woman came rushing toward her, her arms spread wide. "Aunt Tilly," she shouted, and wrapped her arms as far around her aunt as she could, crushing her belly against Matilda, who pulled away.

"You're pregnant," said Matilda.

"I was hoping you wouldn't notice," laughed Beth.

"Married?"

"No," said Beth. "It's just so wonderful to see you. I need to explain it all. Mom and I decided not to tell you about the baby yet."

A nurse approached and said, "She's awake."

"You go see your mother," Matilda said. "I'll be back

later." With that she left her pregnant, unmarried niece, and headed out the door. She sat in her car with her head on the steering wheel.

This was the worst nightmare imaginable—tragedy repeating itself. *How could this be happening again?* Matilda remembered the day when, more or less out of the blue, June, age twenty-two, announced she was pregnant. Later the same day, Matilda broke down at work. She had decided her life was destroyed. She opened her heart to Ethel who rose to the occasion and kindly offered Matilda a place to live, so she moved out of her own house. The two spinsters, as they were known in Morrisdale, lived together in Ethel's apartment. June kept the house.

Ethel was kind and generous, and Matilda loved her, but once they were living together, Matilda realized that Ethel loved her in a different way. Fortunately, there were two bedrooms, and they stayed together, never quite settling into intimacy, and Matilda kept her job. Not having a degree, Matilda could only be assistant librarian, but she ran the place anyway, and Ethel was content to let her smarter, harder working, more competent assistant take over.

Beth was born, and June returned to work. Matilda could not afford to give up the library job, so baby Beth went to day care. After that, except for taking care of Beth whenever possible, Matilda and June lived their separate lives as a matter of choice, living apart in Morrisdale, a few blocks from each other. Matilda did not approve of

June having and raising a child out of wedlock, and June did not approve of Matilda's living arrangements with Ethel. June did not pry, but Matilda knew she had suspicions, just like everyone else in Morrisdale.

Then, slowly, over the years, a sort of rapprochement developed. Beth grew up and moved away. June, with Matilda's assistance, helped Beth make it through college. June softened, and so did Matilda. They even became close again. But then the worst had happened—June's cancer and Beth coming back, pregnant and single.

Matilda's family had started to fall apart when she was sixteen. It had taken all those years for the last thread to unravel. The sister she had raised and finally learned to love unconditionally was slipping away from her again.

Matilda drove downtown and pulled up in front of Phil Neville's travel agency/insurance office. A few days before she'd walked past and been drawn to the cruise posters in his window. Now, she sighed, uncertain. What she told Phil would be shared with his wife and then with everyone else in Morrisdale. She could just imagine Margaret Neville on one of her phone marathons: "Guess who just signed up for a cruise while her sister is dying."

She pulled away, drove back toward the hospice, and then past the hospice and onto the expressway toward the fancy Grant City Mall where she knew there was a Liberty Travel office. "I want a river cruise," she informed the young girl, "in Europe."

"What date?" asked the girl, efficiently poised to write.

"I'm not sure, but soon, very soon."

"Soon?"

"My sister is dying. She's at the hospice in Morrisdale. When she dies I'll have no family—no one. I Just need to get away. It must seem queer that I would take a vacation at such a time."

"It's not that uncommon. I think it's often wise," said the girl who, until that moment, had not seemed particularly insightful. The girl then smiled again and was all business. "So let's just pick a cruise or two, then you call me when you're ready, and I'll get you the earliest possible date. Sometimes there are last-minute openings, and those tend to be really good deals. Just you, is it?"

"There's no one else." Matilda was not about to share a small cabin with Ethel. She was not going through all that again.

"I'm so sorry," said the girl with a new sense of empathy. "I'll find something exactly right for you. I promise."

Matilda spent an hour with the girl at Liberty, then she wandered around the mall and bought a suitcase and a purse that could double as a carry-on for the flight to Europe.

By the time she returned to the hospice it was late afternoon. June was sleeping. Matilda and Beth had tea at the café in the kitchenette set aside for family. Matilda stood at the sink, let the water run until it was as hot as possible, then washed the cup and saucer she had just used. Beth set her cup and saucer next to the sink. Matilda immediately washed those also.

Beth leaned back against the counter, folding her

arms over her huge belly. Matilda said what she was thinking. "You should get back to your hotel. You need to rest." Steam rose to redden Matilda's face, causing a drop of water to condense like dew on the tip of a gray curl that drooped from her forehead. Beth gently reached and touched the drop of water at the end of Matilda's stray curl, taking it onto her own finger. "I know, Aunt Tilly. I just want to be sure you're okay before I leave."

"I'm fine, Beth," said Matilda. She shut the water off with a jerk of her wiry wrist, then wiped a towel on the first cup, which was already dry, the hot water having turned to humidity in the kitchen air. She examined the clean, empty cup, warm in her hand. She was not fine. The sin of planning a cruise as her only sister was dying churned inside her, but what are you supposed to do when a loved one's life is being taken away? She also felt guilty about unburdening herself to the young travel agent. It would've been more appropriate to unburden herself to June's doctor, but she could tell he had absolutely no interest in her story. After putting the last cup on its hook, she met Beth's glance.

"We knew this was coming," said Beth. "Can you sleep?"

"What difference does it make?" Sleep. She knew she would sleep, but sleep, no sleep, Matilda didn't care. At this point, she just wanted it to be over, but she did not say so.

"I'm so sorry, Aunt Tilly," said Beth, giving her aunt a warm hug and a smile before she left her alone. Matilda stared out the kitchenette window and saw only darkness. How could this girl, pregnant and unmarried, be handling her own mother's death better than Matilda herself was, taking Matilda's grief on her shoulders on top of her own. Matilda understood that Beth's life would go on after her mother's death, but Matilda failed to see how her own life could.

Tomorrow, and every day until the end, Matilda would spend the day at the hospice with her sister. June was nine years younger, only fifty, too young to die. June never really knew their parents. All June had known was Matilda, struggling to cope with a boring job, a restless teenager, and a demanding, curly-haired little girl. Being in the hospice revived Matilda's most vivid memory, sitting with ten-year-old June in the Grant City Hospital. Matilda had just turned sixteen when the accident happened.

The next day, Matilda arrived late. She had not fallen asleep until dawn. Beth met her at the door of June's room, looking more pregnant than the day before. They had hoped the baby would be born before June died so she could see her grandchild, but that was at least a month away.

"She's awake, Aunt Tilly," said Beth. "Very alert today. You'll be surprised."

"Is that Matilda?" said June from her pillow. "It's about time."

"Yes, dear," she said as she entered the room and sat next to the bed. "It's me."

"That's Beth's seat," June said. "You sit over here on

the other side of the bed. I've been waiting for you since six a.m. Where were you?"

"Sorry," said Matilda. "I didn't realize you'd be so… so awake."

"They gave me some super shots—lots of morphine. The doctor said I could have all I want. I feel fantastic. This is the first day I can remember when I didn't feel like someone was kicking me in the stomach every ten minutes. I almost feel like I could eat something. I might even drink a glass of water." The three of them chatted and gossiped until noon, and then June suddenly fell asleep. The nurse told them to come back after three.

Once in the lobby, Matilda asked Beth if she'd like to join her for lunch.

"No, thanks," said Beth, "but I'll take you." They left Matilda's car at the hospice, and Beth drove to the Grant City Mall. During the drive they did not talk. Matilda watched the city go by.

They sat in a little Italian restaurant named Guido's that featured red-and-white checked tablecloths and straw-covered chianti bottles. A candle was lit in the center of each table.

"It's so nice to spend time with you, Beth, even under the circumstances," said Matilda. "I have always felt guilty about not taking more of a role in your life."

"Nonsense," said Beth. "You've done a lot for me. I know you helped pay for college. I'm eternally grateful. And I know you're worried about me. It shows, and I appreciate it, but please listen." She reached across the table and gently squeezed Matilda's hand. "I'm fine, Aunt Tilly. I'm going to get married. I have a job. I work at home. I can raise my child. Matt can take time off whenever he wants. We're only a few hours away. If I need you, I know I can count on you."

Matt. His name was Matthew. She'd remember that. They didn't talk much more at Guido's. Matilda felt a lump in her throat, and she was at a loss for words.

When they returned to the hospice, June was awake from her nap, but there was a dramatic change. Her face was ghostly, and she stared straight up from her pillow as if her head could not move. "Hi," she whispered without changing expression. Matilda was sitting in her assigned seat across from Beth. "No," said June, struggling to speak, "move that chair next to Beth so you're both on the same side." Matilda did as she was told, and then she and Beth leaned their heads together over June's pallid face that rested on the white pillowcase.

"That's better," said June, and she almost smiled. "There's something we have to discuss, Matilda. There's something you must do for me."

Matilda stiffened. "Of course," she said.

"I was hoping to see my grandchild but...I feel very tired," she said, and her eyes closed. Beth and Matilda did not move. June's eyes reopened. "Where was I? Oh, yes. A child must have a grandmother."

"Yes, of course, and you will always be her grandmother, June," said Matilda.

"No, Matilda, *you* will be her grandmother."

"I'll be her great-aunt. I'll be the best great-aunt any child ever had. You don't need to worry about that."

"Oh, shut up and listen to me," said June, struggling to lift her head off the pillow. "Who in the world ever cared about a great-aunt? Great-aunts are old biddies, used-up spinsters. Grandmothers are special, and you have to be one for Beth's child. You have to, don't you see?" And her eyes closed again.

Beth and Matilda waited for more, but June had returned to sleep. Matilda reached and gently shook June's shoulder. "Don't," said Beth. "Let her sleep." And Matilda pulled her hand away, embarrassed. She stood and moved to the window. Beth followed and stood beside her.

"Mother told me yesterday what she was going to ask you, and asked me to think about it," said Beth. "And I told her this morning it was a wonderful idea."

"Matt has a mother, of course," said Matilda.

"She doesn't approve of me, and she lives in La Jolla with the rest of the weirdos. His dad's around. They're divorced. He's okay." She glanced at the bed. June was sleeping peacefully. "In fact, he's very anxious to meet my Aunt Tilly. So, you see, the grandmother job comes with a potential boyfriend."

"But Beth," said Matilda, "it would be so unfair. The child will eventually know and feel betrayed. No, Beth, I just can't do it. It would be a lie."

"Well," said Beth, "that's what I said to Matt this morning, and you know what he said? He said yeah, it's a lie, and we have to tell the truth, so I guess our child won't have Santa Claus or heaven or the tooth fairy. Not even a granny. So, basically, he thought it was a hoot. He thinks you're a saint."

"A saint? Ridiculous."

"I told him all about you. Maybe I lied a little. Oh, Aunt Tilly, this is *all* so ridiculous. I guess—I guess I'll have to call you 'Mom.'"

They fell into each other's arms. The nurse burst in upon the sobbing women, glanced at the bed, and said, "Oh, dear. Has she...?"

"No," said Matilda, "just asleep, we think."

Two weeks later the girl from Liberty Travel called to say she had found just the cruise. "I'm so sorry," said Matilda. "I should have called you. I can't do it. I'm expecting my first grandchild this month."

"But I don't understand. You said—"

"I know, but as it turns out, I have more family than I thought."

THE FILMMAKER AND
THE NIGHT WATCHMAN

NEW *idea:* It's based on this guy, Walter, in my building. I don't know his last name. He works at night—a sweet guy. I bet I can get him to do it because I think he has a crush on me.

Opening scene: Night—empty city street—zoom in on illuminated digital clock, orange numbers, reading 4:59 a.m. (I know clocks usually don't say "a.m." or "p.m.," but *this* one does.) As we watch, the clock flashes to "5:00 a.m." A bus pulls up to a bus stop in front of the clock, and a man—Walter—gets on. He carries an old-fashioned metal lunch pail. (He really does.) As we ride the bus with Walter, we watch the night pass slowly by. After work, he is the only passenger, and the bus is pretty much the only traffic. We pass another bus traveling in the same direction, and Walter sees himself reflected in the window of that empty bus. The buses are side by side. His reflection pulls ahead or drops behind as if there were another Walter. The only other living thing we see is a solitary dog—maybe a stray, certainly a mongrel. We zoom in and see the dog isn't wearing a collar. This dog is free—independent, outside the system, yet cautious. All this has to be conveyed in a few seconds. Maybe it's in the dog's eyes. It runs—long legs, tawny under the streetlights—alongside the bus. As the bus speeds up, the camera, now in the bus, stays on the running dog that gradually fades away, unable to catch up. The bus stops at the Ambassador Apartments. We watch Walter from the bus as he enters the dimly lit lobby. *Blackout.*

"You're quiet this morning, Walter," said the bus driver. I was on my way home. It was five a.m.

"I was thinking about the woman in my apartment building, wondering when I would see her again. I haven't seen her in two weeks—fifteen days, actually. I see her when I come home from work. She's just coming down for her morning paper. Sometimes we chat, so I know she's some kind of filmmaker. I thought maybe she was on location somewhere. Her name is Mary."

We rode—only the two of us—the driver and me—in silence. "How come you stop at every stop even when no one is there?" I asked. "At this time of day, no one gets on or off."

"You do," he said, then he smiled, shook his head, and gave me a look. "You know I have a schedule. You know I have to stop at every stop." I knew it was a stupid question. I couldn't even carry on a friendly conversation with a bus driver.

Along the deserted street a dog was studying a hydrant—maybe a stray, certainly a mongrel. The bus stopped. The dog and I stared at each other, and the bus started again.

I was so out of practice in the game of conversation. I liked to talk to Mary, but I always struggled with what to say. I guess I connect better with animals than with people. I told the driver, "I like to watch the city go by."

"Depends on your point of view," he said. "When you sit where I do, it's not so much going by. It comes right at you." Then I looked forward and saw what he meant.

As I got off at my stop, the dog trotted up, panting—a gentle creature. I reached out a hand. The dog barked, backed away, then followed me at a cautious distance.

Second scene: Night again on the city streets.

Zoom in on dog: Same dog from first scene—the dog follows Walter as he walks, but the dog keeps a cautious distance. Walter stops at an all-night coffee shop. The dog hangs around and is still there when Walter exits the coffee shop. Walter holds a plastic cup. Steam rises from the little hole in the lid. Walter tears a piece from his doughnut and tosses it to the dog, who desperately snaps it up and swallows it in a second.

Production note: The dog, of course, is Walter—a stray, a lost soul—a creature of the night—a little afraid, shy. You sense that he needs people but holds himself apart. Human relations are difficult for him. He is gentle, approachable, but when someone does approach him, he backs away.

Tomorrow I'll be home and intend to talk to Walter.

As I got off the bus I went up to my apartment and turned on the TV. I had taped *The Umbrellas of Cherbourg* off TCM. The movie ended, but I had to stay awake in case Mary was back. At seven-thirty I went down to the lobby, and there she was in her robe and fuzzy slippers.

"Hi, Walter," she said as she picked up her newspaper. "Long time no see. How are you?" She smiled. "Work last night?"

I nodded. "I'm good," I said. "And you?"

"Just got back," she said. She didn't say where she'd been. She asked me if she could ask a personal question. I nodded. "What do you do—your job, I mean?"

I looked at her as she smiled at me. She was interested in what I do. "I'm a night watchman."

"I was hoping for that answer, Walter."

I told her I sat in the guardroom of an office building all night watching twenty-six television screens connected to twenty-six cameras, but in all the time I had worked there I had never seen anything—nobody entering, nobody leaving—nothing, ever, on any of the twenty-six screens.

She asked me how I could stand to do that. I thought a moment and then I said, "Well, actually, it's kind of soothing."

She smiled again before she said, "Walter, there's something I'd like to talk to you about—a project—a film project." Then she asked me about the city at night, and we talked for almost ten minutes. Finally, Mary said she had to go up and get dressed for work, and I tried not to think of her getting dressed.

Production notes: Walter has committed to the project.

Notes on Walter: Quiet, nice—night watchman—part of that thin blue line that separates our world from the dark world. I want the film to walk that line. He's a bit of a mystery—assumed he had a working-class background, something like that, but this morning he asked me if I understood Stonehenge. And he told me he taped *The Umbrellas of Cherbourg.* It's one of his favorite movies, he said, and he said "movies" not "films." He said it was soothing to sit and watch twenty-six television screens and never see anything happen. He doesn't talk much, but he used the word "detritus" in our conversation: "When you work at night, you are part of the world's detritus." Intriguing. Should I have him say that in the film? Yes.

She is making a movie of the city at night, a *film noir*. Dark lonely streets. Streetlights. The nocturnal world—a movie of my world. Maybe I'll find out who I really am.

Scene notes: First scene has been shot—about a minute long after cuts. The city at night. Walter walks through the streets at five a.m., and I walk with the camera—behind him or beside him. Sometimes I walk backward, facing him. There is sound—sounds of the few cars that go by, a couple distant sirens, but mostly it's quiet. We walk slowly. It's cold enough to see his breath under the streetlights, which gives the scene a noir look. Sometimes you can see my breath in the frame, which adds atmosphere, makes the air itself palpable, but you never see me. I film in color, but it will look like black-and-white because of the lack of natural light. Some mystery. Some tension. Where is he going? We never find out. *Blackout.*

Production note: Haven't found a dog yet. Walter says there's one around here. After the shoot, after dawn, we were looking for the dog, and Walter asked to take my picture. Made me pose. He wanted the dawn's early light, he said, not behind him, or backlit, but off to the side— "slanted light" he called it. And he said he liked my scarf.

I now have two pictures of her, one in front of a brick wall and one in front of a stone wall. Her hair is the color of the seams and facets of the stone—the color of wheat—and it's silky. Her cheeks—her skin—from pink to cream, the colors of the brick if you added light and smoothness and life. She always wears a scarf that seems carefully chosen. "You seem content—happy in your life," she told me.

"Does that surprise you?" I asked.

Scene: Last night we shot again as we walked through the park. My voice says, "Tell me about the night." Walter walked without talking or responding. There is silence for thirty seconds—a long time in a documentary—as if time has stopped while Walter keeps moving—outside of time—as if the night in the city is outside of time. Then he speaks: "I can remember as a boy being afraid in my bedroom—afraid of the shadows. As I grew older, I remember some nights I would walk home in the dark through the streets of my town. For some reason those walks are vivid in my memory. I cannot picture my school or my friends, but I can picture the streets I walked at night—up Walnut Street, down Main Street, across the park by the war memorial—and then around the corner. I could see the lights at my house and, as I tell you this, I can feel it again, see it again—how glad I was to see those lights. Sometimes in bed I relive that memory, and it makes me feel the quiet. I think that's when I usually fall asleep, just when I see the lights of my house." His voice is soft, natural, like talking to a friend, just right.

Mary and I had several filming times together—all at night. I liked to think about being with her—anticipating—thinking of things to say to her. One night I showed her my favorite all-night coffee shop. The stray dog was there, and Mary was excited and started filming the dog. We tossed it doughnuts. Mary laughed. It was fun.

I wanted to ask her to go back there with me after we finished shooting, but when I was with her I was uncomfortable—nervous the whole time. I didn't know what to say. The wonderful thoughts in my head stayed there or came out like nonsense. I couldn't even say, "Let's have coffee."

Production notes: Found my dog. Walter took me to an all-night coffee shop, and the dog was there. Not what I had hoped for, but a stray, and it works. The dog knows Walter, which is good because we were able to get some shots of the dog following his bus. It was just as I imagined. We fed the dog doughnuts, and now it waits for us at the coffee shop.

One more scene to shoot.

Mary came to my bedroom and filmed me going to bed at seven in the morning. As I relaxed in bed after shooting, she sat next to my bed on the chair where I arrange my clothes for the next day. I wore pajamas for the scene even though I actually sleep in my underwear. It was dark in the room, but she didn't pull up the shade. She told me that was the last scene. The project was over. "Tell me about yourself, Walter," she said. "Where are you from? How did you come to be here?"

There wasn't much to tell, so I said, "I have no history. I'm just here now."

She looked at me and smiled. "I see. There is no backstory. There's just Walter in the here and now."

"Yes."

"Okay. I'll leave you to sleep now, Walter. Do I say good night or good morning?" She smiled and left me, and I closed my eyes and thought of myself heading down Main Street, turning the corner, and seeing the lights of my house.

Scene: Walter's apartment. The early light of dawn flows in the window. The apartment is neat—everything in its place. A few books are piled evenly on a coffee table. There is a couch and one upholstered chair—kitchenette—table with two chairs. It's clean too. His bedroom has a single bed, a nightstand, one wooden chair. Apparently, his favorite color is brown; maybe it's his only color. The bathroom is tiny—the bed is neatly made—tight corners. Walter goes to the window and pulls the shade down and the beige curtains together. A shot of a straight wooden chair in the bedroom with his clothes precisely arranged for his day that begins at 1 p.m. The room darkens. He pulls back the covers, climbs into bed, and pulls the covers over his head. *Blackout.*

Mary was gone for thirteen days, and when she returned, I asked how our movie was coming. "Come on up and see for yourself," she said. Her apartment was filled with clutter—books and magazines everywhere, unwashed dishes, about a thousand pillows all over the place, most everything was red or orange—bright colors. Her bedroom door was open, and her bed was a mess. She moved some things off the couch so I could sit facing the TV. She turned the lights down. There was a bedside light on in her bedroom, and a silk nightgown had been tossed onto the bed.

"This is the premiere," she said, "so we have to have wine." She poured me a glass of Riesling and sat next to me with her own glass in hand and, at seven a.m., we watched the film of me at night.

When the last frame had disappeared, Mary quietly asked, "So, what do you think, Walter in the here and now?"

I told her it was good. "It's part of me."

"There's more?"

I nodded.

"Of course," she said.

It was good—sensitive—but only about the night. The interesting thing was that the star was the stray dog that hangs around the coffee shop. Mary is in there, too, but we never see more than her shadow, and a couple of times we hear her voice. (She says the dog was her idea.) The dog sort of makes me think of her—aloof. It won't come near me. I mean, it comes near, but not too close. I think maybe she sees the dog as herself. That's the kind of thing filmmakers do, and it gives the film meaning and depth. She said she thought I looked content with myself, which maybe I am, but I wonder if she is projecting. I wonder if she's less than happy with herself. She doesn't seem sad, but she is alone.

Last Scene: I don't like it. Walter's day ends at dawn. So what? I don't like the ending where he goes to bed at dawn. I don't think that's who he is. But then who is he? The part of his day when he gets up in the afternoon is the beginning, and it's boring. He leads a backward life, but so do a lot of people. That's not a story. That's not a documentary. Not the way I see it. The viewer must come away with an idea of who Walter is—a stray, a lonely guy, but not *just* a lonely guy—something more. I don't know. Something. What I have is good, but I need one more scene, at least.

I didn't see Mary again for several days. It was getting closer to the time of year when the sun comes up directly at the end of our east-west street. We are four blocks from the river, so looking down our street is like looking toward the end of a long tunnel. The sunrise shifts a little north or south every day, and the next day I knew the sun would come up directly at the end of our street. If the sky was clear, that sunrise would be spectacular.

Mary was in the lobby when I came down to witness that sunrise. She glanced up at me. I told her I wasn't going to bed quite yet; I had to see the sunrise. "It's going to be quite something today, I hope."

"Really? Then I should grab my camera."

I strolled into the gray pre-dawn.

About five minutes later, Mary and her camera joined me. "You seen my dog around?" she asked.

"Yeah," I said, "he's around." I pointed, but not at the dog. I could see an orange glow. The sun was just rising over the East River. Then, in a matter of seconds, the street was filled with blinding brilliance as a shaft of light shot down the street. The pavement turned from gray to gold, and the sensational sunshine filled the end of the street like fire.

"Wow!" was all she could say. For two full minutes Mary and I stood in the soft splendor of those sunbeams until they were bocked or disbursed by awnings, street signs, and traffic lights.

"You knew that was going to happen. How did you know? Is that why you asked me if I understood Stonehenge?"

"Did you catch it with the camera?"

"I don't know. Maybe. Probably not. You know, shooting into the sun . . ." She paused, glancing down at the camera in her right hand. "I need that on film. It has to be in there. This is the final scene that I was missing. I suppose I'll have to wait a year."

"For this street you would," I said, "but the sunrise shifts from block to block every day or so."

Together we strolled into the lobby of our building. She was about to pick up her newspaper when she said, "Yeah," looking at me as if I were a genius, "I bet it does." She smiled. "You say you have no backstory. I like that. At least I think I do. I mean, you haven't been in jail or anything like that, have you? I know you haven't."

"No, I haven't. How about you?"

She smiled. "Well, that's sort of a long story. Want to hear it?"

"Sure. Let's get some coffee."

GHOSTS IN THE HOUSE[1]

"WINE snob," said my sister as she stood next to my open refrigerator door. "You never have any beer." Deborah lifted out a Meursault and took a swig straight out of the bottle. "How can you drink this horse piss?"

"Listen," I said, and I pushed the button on the answering machine to play a message from Aunt Marcia: "Phillip, you cannot sell the house. Call me immediately."

"Well, that's straight to the point," said Deb. "So what are you going to do?"

"Ignore her. Mom died more than six months ago. The house is listed. I don't want it. You don't want it. It can't just sit here. Pour me a glass of that."

"Pour it yourself," she said as she handed me the

---

1 In Illinois.

bottle. "You have to call her. You always avoid confrontation.[2] That's your whole problem. She's our aunt. We can't ignore her. Either you handle it or I will." She grabbed the bottle back and finished the wine in one swallow. "Got any more of this? We'll just pay Aunt Marcia a visit tomorrow. I'll pick you up at noon."

Aunt Marcia uses her "parlor" only for company, and company is rare. Most of the time she sits alone in the kitchen, last remodeled in the seventies, in her "house on the hill," as she calls it, except it isn't.[3]

Deb and I sat on Aunt Marcia's chintz sofa that looks and feels like fabric stretched over plywood with rocks for throw pillows. Deb had hypocritically worn a dress, so I knew she was going to put on an act. Our aunt was wearing a floral dress that looked the same as every other dress I've seen on her. Deb says no one can figure out where she buys them. Although it was lunchtime, she didn't offer us anything to eat or drink, not even a glass of water, which didn't surprise me. I'd never seen Aunt Marcia eat or drink. She probably thinks it's unladylike to eat in front of others. "I was born there, your mother

---

2 This is a lie. I don't rush in like a fool.
3 Actually, it's sort of in a hole.

was born there[4] and lived her entire life there," said Aunt Marcia. "It's our ancestral home."[5]

"Aunt Marcia," I said, "it's a simple matter of necessity. The house can't just sit there."

Aunt Marcia started to cry.[6] "It was always understood that it would be in our generation until your mother and I were gone.[7] I can't stand the thought of someone outside the family living there.[8] Can't you do anything, Deborah?"

Deb stood and wrapped her arms around Aunt Marcia. "I wish I could. Mother left all the decisions to him,"[9] she said with a dismissive nod in my direction. "He can do anything he wants. All I get is a little money that, of course, means nothing to me."[10]

Aunt Marcia shook her head and said, "My little sister was always such a silly fool."

---

4 Notice she doesn't mention their older brother, my Uncle Mort, who was not a bad guy, but he did have a little trouble with the Securities and Exchange Commission and became *nunc pro tunc* nonexistent as far as Aunt Marcia was concerned.

5 My grandfather bought the house in 1936 in foreclosure. Three families and the bank had owned it previously. There are five other houses just like it on the street.

6 Actually, she was dabbing her dry eyes with the stiff linen handkerchief she had for the occasion.

7 Dead.

8 They might be Puerto Rican, or black, or Italian, or German, or Canadian.

9 Another lie.

10 Ibid.

"I'm sorry, Aunt Marcia," I said.

"Well," said Aunt Marcia, "we have to do what we have to do, I guess. The sad thing is that the people who buy this house are going to have to put up with ghosts."

Deb and I looked up, and Deb said, "What ghosts?"

"Why, the spirits of Mother and Father and my dear sister. They won't leave that house until I'm gone. We all promised each other that."[11]

Deb, who had sat back on the plywood divan, returned to Aunt Marcia and wrapped her arms around her again.[12]

"I understand, Aunt Marcia. Don't worry. We'll take the house off the market immediately. Right, Phil?"

"Deb," I said, "that would create a problem. There are taxes to pay and the lawn to mow and all that kind of stuff."

"Well," said Deb, "look at it this way: what if something happened and someone in the family needed a place to live?"

"What are you talking about?" I asked. "Everyone in the family has a place to live."

"Well, I mean, you never know," said Deb. "What if, say, someone just turned up like, say, Uncle Mort.[13]

11 At the time, Illinois Law required realtors to disclose all ghost sightings. I knew it, and Deb knew it, and would Aunt Marcia have brought it up if she hadn't known it? Not likely.

12 This was a world record for Deb hugging Aunt Marcia—two in one day without retching.

13 See footnote 3.

I expect he's still around somewhere. He's family. He'd have a place to live."

"That," said Aunt Marcia, "is absurd."

We made our way up the slight slope from the house on the hill to the road. I kicked the loose gravel as hard as I could. "What's the matter with you?" I asked. "Uncle Mort? He has to be dead by now. Are you crazy?"

Deb looked at me in that superior way she has. "Relax, Phil. Listen: he probably is dead by now, but maybe he isn't, but I bet Aunt Marcia doesn't know for sure. And now, thanks to her, he'll have a place to live, dead or alive."

The next week I got a call from Aunt Marcia; it was all sweetness. She wanted me to sell the house…as soon as possible. "Phillip," she said, "I've changed my mind. You know, Deborah came to see me again, and we had a long talk. I feel good about new people moving into the homestead. I hope you find a nice young family, any family."

I said I was pleased.

"I'm sure you are," she said. "I know it's hard for you to sell the house to strangers, the house you grew up in, but we have to move on. I just can't stand the thought of those family ghosts hanging around. So I told them all to shoo, and they did."[14]

---

14 Blood is thicker than molasses, usually.

THE GOLDFISH WITH LONG BLACK HAIR

"HI, pet."

"Is that you, Daddy?"

"Of course."

"When are you coming home?"

"Not right away, but soon. Don't you worry, sweetheart."

"When?"

"I can't say for sure, but…but let's talk about you. What have you been doing?

"Nothing."

"Anything new? You started school, didn't you?"

"Yeah."

"Tell me about kindergarten."

"It's okay."

"Do you like your teacher?"

"She's okay."

"What's her name?"

"Um, I forgot."

"I see. Well, I'm not sure what else to ask you, pet. I think I have to hang up soon. They only let me talk a few minutes."

"Daddy?"

"Yes, pet?"

"I have a fish."

"A fish?"

"Yes, and his name is Ned. I named him."

"Ned?"

"Yes, he's in a big round bowl called a fishbowl filled with water about this high, and he just swims around. And we have this little orange package with a picture of a fish, and there's dust in it, and we put a little dust in the bowl every day, and it floats, and Ned swims up and makes his mouth like a little kissy-face, and somehow the dust just goes into his mouth, and that's all his food, just fish dust."

"Masie, I really have to go now. There's a man here who says I have to hang up."

"Wait, Daddy, there's more I have to tell you."

"Go ahead, sweetheart. I'm listening."

"And he has a chair to sit in."

"A chair?"

"Yes, he has a chair to sit in and he reads the newspaper."

"The newspaper?"

"Yes. It's a little newspaper. About this big. It's fish size, and it has fish news."

"I see. Just a minute, Masie…(It's my daughter. She's telling me about her new goldfish. He reads the newspaper.) Okay, Masie, the man says we can talk one more minute. Please make it quick."

"He's a very special kind of fish, isn't he, Daddy?"

"He certainly is special if he can read."

"No, Daddy, all fish can read. He's special because he's gold-colored and he has long, black hair."

"Hair? I've never heard of a fish with hair."

"That's why he's unusual."

"Does he comb it?"

"No, he doesn't need to. When he's in his chair it just hangs down, and when he swims it flows behind him."

"I see. Well, Masie, I have to hang up now. I'm allowed to call you once a month and only for a couple minutes. I'll call you next month."

"Where are you, Daddy?"

"I have to go now, sweetheart. I love you."

"I love you too, Daddy. Where are you?"

"Hi, Daddy."

"Hi, sweetheart."

"Daddy, when are you coming home?"

"So how's Ned? Tell me what Ned has been up to."

"Ned?"

"Your goldfish, you know, with the hair."

"Oh, yeah, Ned. He's great."

"That's all? I mean, what have you two been up to? What's the news in the fish newspaper?"

"Well, let me think. Oh, yes, now I remember. Ned's team won the championship, and it was in the newspaper—the fish paper. Yes, it was."

"What championship?"

"Baseball. Ned hit a home run to win the game."

"Wow, that's super. I really can't imagine fish playing baseball."

"Well, it goes slower underwater, and they don't really run, you know. They swim around the bases and…"

"Can you read the fish newspaper?"

"No, silly. It's written in fish, but Ned tells me about it."

"He tells you?"

"Yes. When he talks he makes bubbles, and when the bubbles float to the top they pop and go "blip, blop, blip"—like that—and I can understand it. It sounds sort of like gargling and talking at the same time. I've told him all about you, and he can hardly wait to meet you. He reads the sports news out loud to me, just like you used to do. 'Listen to this, Masie,' he says, and then, when he finishes, he says, 'Now, what do you think about that, Masie girl?' He sounds just like you, Daddy. Remember?"

"I sure do."

"Where are you, Daddy?"

"Hi, sweetheart."

"Hi, Daddy. Mommy told me a little about where you are, so I won't ask anymore."

"I see."

"I know you did something bad, but not that bad, and you have to be in that place for a while."

"That's right, I do. You know it's not as awful as I thought it would be, so you don't need to worry."

"Okay, I won't worry. Daddy?"

"Yes?"

"Does this mean you're not mayor anymore?"

"Yes, I'm afraid it does."

"That's too bad. When will you be home?"

"Well, not for a while. Now tell me, what have you have been doing this month?"

"What's your room like, Daddy?"

"Well, it's, um, basic."

"Do you have your own room?"

"No, I have a roommate."

"Is he nice?"

"Well, that's an interesting question. He's okay. I don't think he was ever mayor of anyplace. I've told him all about Ned, and he said you must be quite a girl. I actually made him laugh. So what's he been up to lately?"

"Who?"

"Ned, your goldfish."

"Right. Ned. Well, lots of fish stuff."

"Still playing baseball?"

"Daddy, don't be silly. It's wintertime. So now he's playing basketball, of course. And he can dunk."

"He can?"

"Yeah. Get it? My fish can dunk."

"I do. I get it."

"And he can dribble with both fins."

"Time's up, Masie."

"Talk to you next month, Daddy. Be sure to tell your roommate about the basketball."

"Hi, Dad."

"How's my girl?"

"Great, Dad."

"How's second grade going?"

"Dad, I'm in third grade now. You know that."

"I'm sorry, Masie. I'm afraid it all runs together."

"I understand, Dad. It's okay."

"Thanks, sweetheart. Now tell me about everything."

"Everything?"

"Well, most importantly, how is Ned?"

"Of course, Ned. Well, let's see. Um, he's growing a mustache."

"Seriously?"

"Yup, seriously. He is. He's grown up now. He's old enough for a fish to grow a mustache."

"I can hardly wait to see it."

"Well, it's kind of a small mustache, Dad. It's hard to see."

"Hello, George."

"Hi, dear. The parole board met this morning. I was sentenced on April 1 three years ago. I walk out of here on the anniversary date. They say I'm a model prisoner."

"I'm sure you are. You fool a lot of people."

"You will take me back, won't you?"

"Mmm."

"I promise you, dear, it won't happen again."

"Sure. I know one little eight-year-old who will be beside herself with joy."

"Of course. Speaking of Masie, how is Ned?"

"Who?"

"Ned, Masie's goldfish."

"Goldfish?"

"The goldfish. The one with long, black hair and a mustache."

"What? Oh, yes, I do remember a goldfish. It came from the school fair. I said it was not a good idea, but Masie was persistent. It was the day after they had walked you out of the courtroom in handcuffs, so what could I say? It came home in a plastic bag and, of course, she overfed it. It lasted about two weeks. When we flushed it down the toilet, she watched it go, cried for about ten minutes, and then wanted another one. I said we'll see, and I never heard another word about it. What's this about long, black hair?"

"Down the toilet. I don't believe it. She kept it going—every month for three years. Incredible. What? What's that noise? You're crying. There's nothing to cry about, dear. I'm coming home."

"I'm not crying, George. I'm laughing."

.   •

IN WHICH WALT WEIGHS 300 POUNDS AND CINDY HAS SEX WITH THE POOL BOY

"OH, Mother," said Timmy, "don't be such an asshole." A twelve-year-old actually said those words to his own mother. If I hadn't been there to see it and hear it myself, I would not have believed it. Cindy scowled at me but said nothing. Nothing! She just ignored it.

Timmy had just come in the back door and hung his backpack in the mudroom. "I thought I told you to come straight home from school" was all Cindy had said.

That morning an even more disturbing event had occurred. A man had come to clean the pool. Actually, he was a boy—couldn't have been more than twenty. He was upstairs with Cindy for an hour. I was downstairs the whole time. That was when my sleepless nights began.

Why does a woman with a husband and family have

sex in the morning with the boy who comes to clean the pool? Why does she hurt the ones she loves? Why does a well-raised adolescent suddenly call his mother names to her face? Why does he hurt her—on purpose? This family has empathy for one another. I've seen it. So why do they hurt each other? It troubles me because it seems a key part of the somewhat more profound question of what underlies human behavior. Why do nice people do bad things to each other? If something could shed light on that issue, maybe we would be a step closer to solving the mystery of why there is evil in the world.

At the time those thoughts were fermenting in my brain, Ambrose and I were in bed. He was asleep. It was way past midnight, so the rest of the family was asleep upstairs. I had not slept a wink. I was trying to get comfortable—trying to stop thinking about Timmy or the pool guy. Maybe if I shifted my legs.

"Stop fidgeting," said Ambrose.

"Are you awake?" I asked.

"I am now," he said, turning to look at the clock on the kitchen microwave that was visible from our bed. "My God, Ginger, do you realize it's two a.m.?"

"I'm sorry. I can't sleep."

"You need to get used to this. People just do what they do. Stop trying to understand them."

"I suppose, but how could she do this? When she and the pool boy came back downstairs, I could smell it."

"How vivid," said Ambrose.

"I can't help it. I *could* smell it. This family is falling apart. I can't just brush it off the way you do."

"I know that pool kid. He's an artist. He and Cindy talk about art. Maybe that's what they were doing upstairs."

"I don't think so."

"Neither do I," said Ambrose. "Anyway, I don't just brush it off, but I don't obsess about it either. I need to sleep, and so do you."

"I can't help it, Ambrose. I worry, and I can't sleep when I worry."

He sighed. "I understand, Ginger. We're different. You worry, but really, what's the point of worrying about things beyond your control? In ten years you and I will be dead and gone, and they will still be living their passions, doing what humans do."

"Thanks, Ambrose. That's really a comforting thought. I'll be dead in ten years. I feel so much better."

"Go to sleep."

I was quiet for a minute, then I said, "The other night, Walt came downstairs at three o'clock."

"Yes, Ginger, I heard him too."

"He had a glass of milk and a huge handful of Oreos, which he is not supposed to eat. He's over three hundred pounds now," I said. "He sat on the couch in the dark. I got up and went over to him. He held me on his lap."

"I know. You woke me up twice that night."

"Ambrose, he was crying. He held me on his lap and

cried in the middle of the night. I wish there was something more I could do."

"Ginger, believe me, you're doing all you can. Now,
shut up. I'm going to sleep." He curled up between my
legs, and in less than a minute, I heard his gentle purring
and felt his soft little body against mine.

Walt and Cindy Johnson have a beautiful big house in the
suburbs with a big yard. They were raised in what I'd call
luxury, and both come from happy families. Both sets of
parents visit us often.

Ambrose and I have had much harder lives. We both
spent time in shelters, and neither of us has any idea
where our parents are. Who knows where either of us
would have ended up if Walt and Cindy hadn't taken
us in?

When I first arrived, I slept in Timmy's room. Timmy
was a little afraid of the dark, but not when I was there.
Ambrose slept in April's room. There was a bedtime rou-
tine. Every night they read a chapter of *Winnie the Pooh*
to Timmy. His parents took turns, first Walt, then Cindy.
Cindy was a great reader. She did all the voices. She made
Winnie sound like Winston Churchill because, she said,
that's who he really was.

At first I thought Ambrose and I had dropped into
the Hundred Acre Wood. This was the ideal place. We
played in the big yard with Timmy and April, and Walt

and Cindy took care of us. We went on picnics and played Frisbee on the beach.

But then bad things started to happen, and the problems snowballed. Walt started gaining weight. Cindy started flirting with the bag boys at the supermarket. Timmy started talking back to his mother.

Ambrose and I love the Johnsons, and they are wonderful to us. Cindy and Walt are educated people. Neither Ambrose nor I have any education but, in a lot of ways, I think we are smarter than they are.

"What's this mess we got ourselves into?" I asked Ambrose. "Instead of the Hundred Acre Wood, it now looks like we're all poor little lambs lost at sea."

"Bah, bah, bah," said Ambrose. "Not all of us, Ginger. Not you and me. Walt and Cindy went to college, and see where it got them. They can read big books. They got learning. We went to the school of hard knocks and got knowledge. It is what it is, Ginger. Ten years from now they will all still be here, and you and I will be gone and forgotten like the rest."

"You already said that. Timmy calls his mother an asshole. Why can't he be like Christopher Robin?"

"Because, Ginger, Christopher Robin is not real. Timmy is real. This is real life, not *Winnie the Pooh*."

"You're telling me."

You may be wondering about the sleeping arrangement—I mean, the arrangement that Ambrose and I sleep together, and the Johnsons don't seem to care. Believe me, it has nothing to do with evil or passion. Walt and Cindy Johnson have two children—April, sixteen, and Timmy, twelve, which constitutes the household, with the exception of Ambrose and me. Technically, we aren't part of the family because we're not people.

Ambrose is a tabby tomcat with subtle gray stripes. My name is Ginger. I'm a dog—a thirty-pound, sort of lazy, lovable bitch without papers. Two years ago, Walt and Cindy liberated me from the local animal shelter. I am thought to be about five years old. I think that's about right. Ambrose just showed up one day and was welcomed by all, including me. Cindy and Walt are welcoming people. In a warm corner of the family room is my L.L.Bean denim dog bed. Ambrose and I sleep together on my bed for warmth, companionship, and nightly conversation.

I've always had trouble sleeping. I have bad dreams about the shelter. We were warm there, and we were fed there, but our kind was systematically killed there too. That fact brought us together. We got along with each other. Every day some of us would be taken out for a walk and never come back. We knew some of us would be gone the next day, but we were helpless. If we made a sound, we knew we were on their list. Can you imagine having to act cute twenty-four hours a day or die?

I explained it to Ambrose: "At the shelter there was a

dog called Cuddles. He told me he had bitten his master, a boy Timmy's age. He said he knew it was a mistake. Cuddles should have been adopted, but he never got out."

"What happened to him?" asked Ambrose.

"He went for a walk."

Ambrose hung his head. "You know what happens to us cats? Our odds are much worse. Once we're in the shelter, we almost never get out."

One week the pool boy came twice. Timmy had pretty much mastered the art of responding to anything his mother said with silence or one-word grunts. It was a storm spinning out of control—more sleepless nights for me. I could see that things were not going to change. Cindy was set on a path. Character is fate, no matter what we do. I learned that at the shelter. I could feel the good times ending and the impending tragedy of a broken home. I wished I knew how to cry.

"Ambrose," I said, nudging him gently with my leg.

"God, Ginger, what is it now?"

"I've been thinking. Things are not changing. Sleeping with the pool boy—calling your mother an asshole—those are things I just can't process. I'm not any closer to understanding what's going on in this house."

"Just enjoy the mystery, Ginger. It's the human comedy."

"I can't be blasé the way you are. I can't put my fears aside. It's not in me. What do you think about us leaving—you and me together?"

"It's a tempting thought, Ginger. I've considered it myself. Every night when they let me out, I try to kill something and eat it, just to be sure I can still do it. I know I could survive."

I shuddered. "I don't think that would work for me."

"Of course not. You couldn't make it, Ginger. Face it. You've surrendered to domesticity. You'd be back in the shelter in two weeks, only then you wouldn't get out. Two-timers don't get out. Anyway, I'm not leaving, and neither are you; they need us here."

"Surrender? I didn't surrender to domesticity. I'm a dog, Ambrose. I'm domestic by definition."

I got to thinking about the domestic thing. Ambrose told me he escaped from the shelter, and although I didn't say so, I didn't believe him, but maybe he did. Maybe that's what Cindy is doing—refusing to surrender to domesticity.

We have a lot of feelings that we can't control. Dogs can't. People can't. Even cats can't. There are other feelings besides empathy. I suppose Cindy's intimate life with Walt has gone awry now that he's fat, and her cute little baby boy is now an obnoxious adolescent. Sweet April is a sullen teenager. Perhaps Cindy was feeling unappreciated, fighting loneliness, looking for love and attention in all the wrong places. Maybe she was facing the choice of being lost or doing something about it—trying to lead her own life—exercising her free will.

We waited. One night, April came down for milk and Oreos, and *she* was in tears. She woke us both up and held us both close to her on the sofa. After I had gulped the Oreo she gave me, she hugged me hard and said, "Ginger, I need you next to me tonight. I need to hug you. I know you love me. I know you care. I know you're worried about me, and that means everything. You can help me get through this. You'll always be my friend. I know that, and I will never forget you. I will always love you." She was hugging me, and I could feel her warm tears on my neck.

Then she turned to Ambrose and said, "Oh, Ambrose, I can tell that you're wondering why I'm like this tonight. I can't help it. I know that if you were me, you would know the answer. Sometimes I do things, and I don't know why I do them. I'm weak. You give me strength. You give me the power to think that maybe I can overcome this, that maybe if I pull myself together, maybe if I stand up for myself, if I'm independent...Oh, Ambrose." And she held Ambrose on her lap and started hugging the breath out of the poor little cat.

Finally, April went back to bed, and so did Ambrose and I. "Well," I said, "that makes the disaster complete. Now April has fallen apart too."

"Cheer up, Ginger," Ambrose said. "Don't you see, she's figured it out? She came to us, not her mother. She knows about the pool boy, or at least she suspects it. She's planning on running away, you know. I saw her packing today and hiding her suitcase."

I had seen her packing as well, but I had thought nothing of it. "God, Ambrose," I said, "what if she does run away?"

"She won't go far—just far enough to scare the daylights out of her parents—and her brother too."

I sighed. "I wish I could share your sanguine attitude."

Ambrose placed a soft paw next to my snout and touched my cheek. "Ginger, you know, you could be wrong. Maybe character isn't always fate. Sure, there's evil in the world, but maybe there's some good too. These things take time. It's also said that guilt comes later, after passion is spent. Then comes remorse."

With that, Ambrose snuggled against my belly and fell asleep.

For a while, nothing much happened.

I took Walt on long walks. He started dieting.

One hot summer day the pool kid came in the back door, without even a knock, and patted me on the head. Cindy appeared. "We need to talk," she said and led him outside. I watched from the window as they sat by the pool talking for about an hour. Then she sat and watched him clean the pool. I watched the whole procedure from the kitchen window. Cindy just sat there in silence. As soon as the pool boy left, she came back into the kitchen, knelt down, and gave me a hug around the neck for longer than usual, pulled back, and looked straight into my face, her hands gently rubbing my ears. "Well," she said, "that's that."

She showed up in the kitchen at two a.m. and poured herself a glass of milk. She poured it into one of the glasses they use for Scotch. She sat on the couch next to our bed. I peeked up at her so she knew I was awake.

"You know, Ginger, you're my best girlfriend—my only girlfriend." She held the glass up to her lips and tipped it toward me. "You never judge me. Ambrose, he looks at me. I can tell he knows what's what. He goes out catting every night too. You don't try to change me. You don't disapprove," she said.

She had it backward, of course, but it didn't matter. "I'm done with that kid. He'll go far. He thinks I broke his heart, but I didn't. If I hadn't let him go, he would have broken mine. Anyway, I couldn't hold him back any longer. I'm going to give them all a chance—one more chance—and try to be a wife and mother. It just might work this time because now they know the stakes. They know what I'll do because I did it. And if it doesn't work, I'm leaving—all of them—except you, Ginger. I'll take you. You and I together will set the world on fire. Think about it." She washed the glass, put it away, and went back to bed. Ambrose slept through the whole thing.

Cindy stayed. Following April's seventeenth birthday party,

which was a huge success, it was after midnight when we all finally got to bed.

"Good night, Ambrose," I said. "You were right. Things turned out so well, didn't they?"

"Of course. You know, Ginger, I know you think I know everything, and you know nothing. What can I say?"

"You could say that I'm wrong."

"Go to sleep, Ginger."

Ambrose says character is fate only on stage, and then only in the tragedies, not the comedies. Is life comedy or tragedy? Or both? Maybe Ambrose's fate was to be gassed at the shelter, but he escaped. Will Cindy escape? It certainly was clear where she was headed, and it's not so clear that she has escaped.

Here is my vision: In ten years, when Ambrose and I are gone and Timmy is a grown man, Cindy will go to the shelter, find the next iteration of me, and the two of them will take off together. I hope they do. I'll be there in spirit.

KAPLAN'S FURNITURE STORE

DELORES Molesworth has visited Kaplan's Furniture store more than a hundred times this year, but she has never bought a thing. Even so, Mr. Kaplan—Herman— always gives her his full attention. That's the kind of person he is. She likes him and wishes she could buy something, but nothing can change in her house.

Jimmy Crawford is the one who counts her visits. Jimmy is Mr. Kaplan's sole employee. He manipulates the pile of rugs when a customer wants to look at the one on the bottom, and he takes over when Mr. Kaplan isn't there, which is not often.

Mr. Kaplan and Jimmy have arranged the furniture in the store to look as it would in a home, so there are several "living rooms" spread around the store. Mr. Kaplan and Mrs. Molesworth always sit in one of those room arrangements. One day last week they were seated on a couch. Mr. Kaplan had lit the floor lamp because they were near the back of the store in their favorite living room. While she was there a few customers appeared, but Jimmy accommodated them. Whatever their business, Mr. Kaplan was not needed.

Mrs. Molesworth was saying to Mr. Kaplan, "You know, Herman, for me, it's the simple things in life. Life is just full of happy surprises for me." He nodded and smiled. "I am content with the mysteries of the world. I'm entranced. Nothing spoils magic more than knowing how the trick is performed. It ruins the miracle. Maybe some people say I have no curiosity. That would be wrong. I want more magic, more mystery. I'm trying to bring Frank around to my way of thinking." Frank is her husband. "He's always in his shop, trying to figure out how those clocks work. I say, 'Frank, be content; enjoy the clocks. Let them do their thing. We don't have to know everything.'"

When she first started visiting the store, maybe the first ten times or so, she and Mr. Kaplan spent time examining carpet samples and discussing her decorating plans, but they also began, like the walrus and the carpenter, to talk of many other things. Mr. Kaplan was a good listener, and so was Mrs. Molesworth. After a while, Mr. Kaplan began to understand the lay of the land. Now they are past talking furniture. They exhausted that subject months ago and have moved on to deeper waters.

Delores dresses impeccably and with taste. Purple is her favorite color. Her tailored suits are modest, maybe a little dated, and perhaps over-dressy for a furniture store. She always has a fresh flower pinned high on her left shoulder, often a rose. Her makeup is discreet and shows signs of careful application.

Herman wears a shirt and tie every day, although he is not an impeccable dresser. Sometimes his shirt and tie are a questionable match, but he is always neat. He has a tie with a picture of a cabin in the woods with smoke curling out of the chimney that billows up to the knot at his neck and amuses Mrs. Molesworth. She told him she likes that tie and, after receiving the compliment, he wears it proudly once a week.

Mr. Molesworth spends most of every day working on his clocks in his basement workshop. If he's not there, he's out looking for clocks, according to Mrs. Molesworth. Mr. Kaplan suggests to Jimmy that Frank is silent at the meals Mrs. Molesworth so carefully prepares for him, except when there has been a major change in his world, such as the acquisition of a new clock or the rare restoration of one that had stopped years ago.

Mr. Kaplan and Jimmy exchange nods or smiles whenever Mrs. Molesworth says, "I hear some of the darnedest things," which she often does. And they smile when Herman reminds her that he gives a five-year floating guarantee on all the carpeting, which is his idea of a joke, but she never seems to get it.

She tells them in detail what her husband likes to eat—in some cases reciting an entire recipe—but there is never much detail about the clocks because, she says, Frank works alone, and she never visits his workshop.

Aside from his clock hobby, which Mrs. Molesworth describes as his "clockwork," the twist of which Mr. Kaplan enjoys, Frank takes two drives twice a week. One takes him past the first house he built, including the guest room above the garage that he and Mrs. Molesworth never used. The Sullivans live there now. Frank built the house from scratch, even leveling the ground for its post and beam construction. Over a span of two years, Mr. Molesworth pounded every nail and sawed every board on weekends and evenings. Mrs. Molesworth says he finished just before the accident, but Frank himself can't even remember what year that was anymore. She supposes he couldn't build anything now—a shed maybe, but nothing more complex than that. She says he parks up the street, sits in the car for a while, and studies the house he built. Then he drives home. The whole ritual takes less than an hour.

Frank's other drive is on poker night. He plays Thursday evenings in Jimmy Crawford's garage, even in the winter, thanks to Jimmy turning on his little electric heater. Jimmy backs the car out of the garage, sets up a table with folding legs, and brings out the kitchen chairs. The garage is attached, which allows them to go from the garage to the kitchen to grab beer and pretzels without encountering the *vicissitudes of the season*. According to Jimmy, they also change seats in the winter because someone is always a little too hot and someone too cold.

In the summer it's always nice and cool no matter where they sit.

At poker, they like to discuss the old days, which is good because Frank will talk about the days before the accident, which he can remember, but he won't talk about the days since. The boys seldom bring up topics from after the accident, and they never discuss his wife's visits to the furniture store.

Frank always leaves poker early. Jimmy says the boys talk about him after he leaves, about how he has changed since the accident. He fell twenty feet onto the concrete floor at the car shops and broke his back. It took two years to recover, but his doctor says he can never return to work, so he went on permanent disability. The boys always have to be careful to let Frank win at poker—just a little; too much and he'd be suspicious. They've learned the hard way that, if he loses, he gets so down on himself they can't stand to be around him.

Mrs. Molesworth is kind of a joke in the neighborhood. She spends a lot of time feeding the birds and the squirrels. Some of the squirrels will take food right out of her palm. That irritates people because they consider the squirrels pests and, by feeding them, Mrs. Molesworth makes them totally unafraid of people. Others say she is weird because most days she is all dressed up, by which they mean she wears a suit and hat.

So it's the neighborhood consensus that Mrs. Molesworth is kind of nutty and empty-headed. Everyone feels sorry for her because of her husband's accident and because he transformed into an ornery guy who is extremely sensitive, one who must be difficult to live with. He complains that the kids in the neighborhood are always whooping and hollering which, of course, they are because they are kids.

Jimmy says everyone thinks Dolores is nutty because she is always happy and smiling even though all she does is feed the birds and squirrels, visit the furniture store, and take care of her difficult, depressed, nervous husband.

But Mr. Kaplan knows it goes deeper, that there is a darkness inside her. He knows Mrs. Molesworth's deep anguish, but he never lets on. He is, perhaps, more serious than necessary, but for him the seriousness is crucial. So he and Dolores engage in conversation that only seems light and directionless. He understands they are playing a deadly game as he struggles to head every uncertainty toward promise.

One day in the store, sitting in their favorite living room, Dolores brought up the squirrels. "They are fascinating," said Mrs. Molesworth. "They live in the moment—there is no past—they play—they chase each other—they chatter to each other—so they do think and talk. They do mate. I watched one pair, and one morning they ran across the road together, but only one made it; the other was flattened by a truck. The survivor, later that same day, was chattering, chasing, and playing with another squirrel."

"I suppose they have no memory," said Herman.

Delores thought for a moment before she said, "No, Herman, they remember. And they plan. I give them nuts, and they bury them, and I've seen them remember where they were buried and dig them up. I couldn't do that. I couldn't even remember which tree I built my nest in. They just accept death as something that happens."

"Maybe it's sadness they lack," said Herman, "remorse."

"Or guilt."

"Maybe they have the feelings and emotions they need to survive but not the ones they don't need, like sadness. Who needs sadness?"

"Maybe," said Delores, "but I like a sad movie, at least now and then."

"Yes, there is that," said Herman, and they gazed at each other. She offered a wistful smile and lifted her eyebrows. Herman loved the delicate sadness of Delores Molesworth.

Whoever sees her on Main Street remarks that Mrs. Molesworth is going furniture shopping because it is known that she always ends up at Kaplan's Furniture Store chatting with Mr. Kaplan. To "do some furniture shopping" has acquired another meaning—an unkind meaning—so in the local bars one guy will say to another, "Done any furniture shopping lately, Fred?"

It has taken some time, but that scurrilous meaning finally worked its way around to Herman Kaplan, and he understands that it is probably connected to the fact that

Mrs. Molesworth has not been to the furniture store for more than a week.

For Mrs. Molesworth, it has been a difficult time. Since her father died, she takes Frank to her mother's house and cooks dinner on Saturday nights. It works out as long as Frank is there. By that she means sometimes Frank is not mentally there, which happened last Saturday. He wandered around his mother-in-law's well-appointed home as if it was all new to him, picking up candlesticks and studiously examining the pictures on the wall, although he had been there every week for years. He picked at his favorite meal, her pot roast and mashed potatoes, as if it might be poison.

Dolores' mother called her Sunday morning to say she had an opinion on the situation. "He's turned into a weak, helpless child—not even a child. He doesn't even know you anymore. He can't operate the television. He takes clocks apart. That's all he does. You need to leave him, Delores. You are entitled to a life of your own. I'll help you through it. I'm not going to give up on this. And stop spending time in that damn furniture store. People are talking. Your behavior is exasperating." Mrs. Molesworth knew better than to argue with her own mother, so she just listened.

Of course, that wasn't the first time such drastic action had been suggested. She and Frank used to go to church, but they don't anymore. One day, about a year after Frank's accident, Reverend Foster took her aside and suggested that she stop going to the furniture store and talking to Mr. Kaplan.

When her mother said she was exasperated, Delores realized that's what Frank has—exasperation—every waking moment he's exasperated. That's his disease, his condition—he tries but is unable to fix the clocks—he can't remember—his injured brain is always struggling just to stay in the real world—sometimes he's there and sometimes he's gone and then he returns—he knows he's back—he knows he's been gone, but he doesn't know where.

Today, Herman and Jimmy are opening the store. "It's been over a week now," says Jimmy, turning on the lights. "The next visit will be number one hundred eleven, just this year. She must be sick or something. Imagine, missing an opportunity to get away from Fluffhead Frank."

Herman adjusts a throw pillow. "I'm afraid, Jimmy; I fear it might be something else. This town has been hard on her. Yet through it all, she still loves Frank, I think. She loves what once was there. Maybe she sees bits and pieces of what's left. I don't know. She keeps looking for the man she loved, and even though he's standing right there, he's a million miles away. It's enough to break your heart, but hers is made of sterner stuff. She keeps hoping."

Jimmy folds his arms and rubs his chin. "You really think she still loves him, Herman? Do you suppose they still do it? You know what I mean." He smiles. "I mean, she's always so cheerful. There must be a reason."

Herman punches the pillow, folds his arms, and glares at Jimmy, but he says nothing. He has also wondered if she and Frank have sex. He hopes they do, but he has decided they probably do not—not since the accident. There is his back, of course, and they would have to talk about clocks, which is a highly unsexy subject. And Frank is always so nervous and depressed that Herman thinks sex with Frank would require Dolores to initiate the action, and he doesn't think she would.

She's never been away for more than a week. He adjusts his tie, ready to greet the first customer of the day. He will miss her. He fluffs another chintz pillow. He admires the way she made herself a world out of the material given her.

At the moment, Frank Molesworth is in the basement, puzzling over a mainspring as if he has never seen one. Meanwhile, Delores Molesworth is upstairs at her dressing table, a fresh pink rose pinned to the shoulder of her suit, making sure her lipstick is perfect.

THE LIBERATION

THE bicycle was dangling over the curb next to a light pole, the handlebars were facing the wrong way, and the front wheel was mangled. A police helmet, the headlamp still lit, rested undisturbed in the middle of the road. Then I saw the body—legs on the curb, head in the road, a member of the Elite Guard lying in a pool of blood in front of the house next door.

Trembling, I closed the blinds. We were in the wrong place, but my wife, my son, and I, as innocent as we were, sat and waited, knowing there was no other choice. To run would signify guilt.

In less than an hour, a van removed the body, the bicycle, and the helmet, then a truck arrived with a crew of two men in white overalls who washed the blood off the road. During all that time, no one had left their homes.

An hour later, several more trucks arrived with their

red-and-blue lights flashing, and everyone on the street was taken to the new Bokali Prison, named for our Liberator. At the prison door I was led away and did not see my family or my neighbors for more than a year.

The guardsman who was killed had bicycled past our house three times a night for months, making sure the curfew was obeyed. The single rifle shot could have been fired from any house on the street. We were all suspects.

I was tossed into a cell with a man named Albert. He had been in prison since before Liberation. He had killed his wife. He said Bokali Prison was a lot nicer than the old one.

While I waited to be questioned, I got to know Albert. He gave me advice. When I complained to him about the wait, he said, "You don't want to be in a hurry." He explained that the New Regime, being short of police, decided it had to resort to the Old Regime's effective system of solving crimes. The system was simple: torture the suspect until he confessed or was beaten senseless. If he confessed, the crime was solved; if not, he was probably innocent and was released. And even if he wasn't innocent, he had learned a valuable lesson he could share.

"Above all," Albert added, "avoid solitary." Albert had never been in solitary. He knew of a few guys who had, but he'd talked to only one, James Krakmayer, a lifer. James told Albert how dark it was and how the silence was even worse than the darkness, but Albert said it was hard to believe. "The crazy guy said he'd been in solitary for over a year, and we all knew it had only been five days." Then there was Freddie "The Thumb" King; he'd been in for three days, but he always said he'd never been in solitary at all.

I was in Bokali for almost a year before they questioned me. The whole time I had no idea where my wife and son were.

When they finally showed up to question me one morning, I was stripped naked and ushered into a brightly lit room that was bare of furniture. Five men stood around me. They told me I was the chief suspect because they never found my rifle. The main questioner asked, "Where did you bury it?" I told them I never owned a rifle. Then another man smashed his fist into my face and kneed me in the groin. I rolled onto the icy concrete floor in horrific pain. As they kicked me, they told me they would kill my wife and son unless I confessed. Then they just kept beating me. The questioning and beating and kicking lasted all day.

Then they threw a blanket around me and dragged me to the commandant's office. I could only open my eyes a slit. I was nearly blind. The commandant glanced at me and quickly looked away, shading his eyes with his hand. "My God, what did you do to his face? This is not the Old Regime."

"He's clean, commandant," said the man who had done the most damage to my face.

"What have I told you about the face?" said the commandant. "I've got a member of the President's Council coming tomorrow. We can't send him anywhere looking like this."

"I'm sorry," said the man who had punched me in the face.

"It's all right," said the commandant, who still couldn't bear to look at me. "Just get him out of here. He's ruining my appetite. Put him in solitary where no one can see him."

"For how long, commandant?"

"We'll see."

They dragged me down several flights of stairs and turned me over to a guard I had not seen before. He was so strong that he held me up with one arm and whispered, "Now, I have to kick you." And he gave me a violent kick in the ass that sent me flying into the darkness.

For a long time I lay on the stone floor. The pain reverberated throughout my body. I thought some bones must be broken. Even if I remained motionless, the pain rushed over me in waves. I hoped I would die. Finally, I passed out.

When I came to, I opened my eyes, but there was nothing to see except utter darkness. Even after what Albert had said, I wasn't prepared for it. I held my hand an inch from my eyes but could not see it. Then there was the silence. The last sound I had heard was the door slamming behind me.

I was afraid to move, afraid I would run into something or plunge into a void. I waved my arms one at a time and crawled, inching my way along. I could not walk. I felt my way around the room, found the walls and the cell door again, which was nothing but a crack in the wall. I estimated that the room was about six paces from wall to wall one way and seven paces the other. Across from the door was a wooden bench attached to the wall. There was no mattress, no pillow. There was a pail in one corner. I had the blanket they had covered me with. That was all.

In my cell with Albert there had been light and noise all the time. Even in the middle of the night there was some noise and enough light to see shadows and silhouettes and, of course, I had Albert. They let us have books, pencils, and paper. Now I was naked and alone. I had nothing.

I found my way to the bench and crawled onto it. I sat in the deafening silence and the abject darkness. When I held my breath and sat still, there was a complete absence of sound. It was so dark I could feel it closing around me. I had known it was going to be dark and silent, but knowing it and experiencing it are two different things.

I realized that if I sat in a certain position there was no pain, only a dull ache. I sat and stared at nothing and lost all sense of time. It seemed like I had been there forever; maybe it was only a day, but it could have been two. I didn't know. All I knew was that I was hungry and cold.

Eventually, the dark and the silence and the cold and the loneliness and the hunger and the nothingness overwhelmed me. I collapsed into self-pity, and I wept.

I wept about my wife and my son and my helplessness until, finally, I lost any sense of consciousness. I believe I wept in my sleep.

When I woke I did not move. I lay there on the bench, unsure if I was alive or dead. If I was alive, I guessed they were going to let me starve to death in the darkness. Time in its usual sense had ceased to exist. It had become a mysterious, hypothetical concept that was absent from my existence.

The only sound was generated by my breathing or my movements. If I shifted in my sleep, I woke myself up with the noise, no matter how otherwise insignificant that sound would have been.

After a long time—whether it was several hours or a few days I will never know—I heard a new sound. It seemed to be coming from the other side of the door, a click maybe. I rolled off the bench, crawled to the door, and felt all around until I located a crevice large enough for me to insert my finger. By doing so I was able to slide open a small door I had not detected before. There was a metal cupboard on the other side at floor level, and I felt inside it. It was about a foot square and a foot high. Inside was a tin plate and water in a tin cup. It was only a small hunk of bread and a half cup of water, just enough to keep me alive. Even though I was desperately hungry, I decided I would save the bread and water as long as I could.

I returned to the wooden bench, placed the bread and water next to me, and waited for what I thought was a long time. I covered myself with the blanket, but I was still cold. I drifted asleep, and when I woke up I was famished and dying of thirst. I couldn't help myself. I ate the bread in two bites and drank the water in a single gulp. I lay down and slept again. I woke up still cold, still starving, and still thirsty, so I crawled to the little food door, but there was nothing. There was no bread. There was no water. I returned the tray and the cup and closed the door.

I dozed off again only to be awakened by a roar like the one you hear when you hold a seashell to your ear, except it kept getting louder and louder until the roar engulfed me as if I were standing next to a huge waterfall or a jet engine.

I stared into the darkness and saw a giant, dark wave moving toward me, growing larger and larger, and I knew if it reached me, I would drown. I closed my eyes, held my hands over my ears, and cowered, expecting to be washed away.

But nothing happened.

When I opened my eyes, I was again greeted with blackness and silence.

I was sweating despite the cold. I wrapped the blanket around me and shivered. I kept staring at where the wave had been, afraid it would return. After a long time, I fell asleep sitting up.

When I awoke, cold and hungry as usual, I crawled to the little door and found bread on the tin plate and water in the cup. I ate the bread and drank the water, but

I was still hungry. I put the plate and tin cup back and rested on the bench for a long time. I knew what they were trying to do. And I knew they would keep me in solitary until I was broken.

Eventually, I fell asleep again. When I woke up, I crawled to the door. The empty plate and the empty cup were still there and still empty.

The whole cell smelled like the pail, which now smelled like my shit, and I lay on the bench for a long time. I realized I was the only person in the world. There was no light, and there was no sound except the deafening silence. There was only blackness—the sound of blackness, the smell of blackness, and the feel of blackness, and I knew I wasn't going to make it. Maybe I already was crazy; I knew the noise and the waves were not real, but they *were* real because I could hear them and see them. I didn't know if it was day or night or if I had been there one day or a few hours or several weeks. I went to sleep cold and hungry, afraid of what I was going to hear in the silence and see in the darkness.

When I woke the next time, I crawled to the door and found bread and water. I ate, but I was still hungry and cold as I sat on the bench knowing the silence would become louder and louder and that the wave would come again, so I sat with my eyes closed, hoping I wouldn't see the wave. I threw the blanket over me; I could almost cover my whole body if I curled into a fetal position. I covered my ears with my hands so I might not hear the silence, and I curled up as close to the wall as I could and tried to think about nothing, nothing, nothing.

After a long, long time I woke up, and I ached all over. I decided I must be sick. I uncovered my ears, and I heard the roar of silence. I kept my eyes closed, slithered off the bench, and crawled to the door. There was bread and water, so I took it and crawled into the corner where I was assaulted by the stench of my own shit.

I decided to save the bread and water. I set them on the bench and crawled around the room again with my eyes closed. I moved slowly, infinitely slowly. I felt every inch of the floor. In one corner there was a crack between the floor and the wall, and I felt something in the crack. I dragged the object out of the crack with my fingernail. It was round and smooth. I stood, carried it to the bench, and caressed it.

It was amazing that I had found anything. I had no idea how it got there. It was impossible for such an object to be where it was, for this thing to be found in that unlikely place. It was real, something I could feel. It was a button.

I put it to my nose. It smelled cold and felt smooth, and I detected four small holes in the center.

It was about half the size of a dime. One side was flat and smooth. That side would lie against the shirt. But there was no thread. There was only the button. The other side had a ridge around the outside, like the ridge on a dinner plate. The outside of my button was thicker than the center where the holes were. I could feel that with my thumb. It seemed to be a perfect circle.

I wondered what color it was and what it was made of. I opened my eyes and held the button up, but I could not see it. It was probably just plastic, but it seemed too smooth for plastic—maybe it was ivory or mother-of-pearl.

I tapped the button on the wooden bench, and it made a noise. I tapped it on the wall, and it made a different noise—a real noise. I held it between my thumb and index finger, and the two sides were different, one smooth and one curved—I think the word is concave. I placed the button next to my head, and I slept for a long time.

I woke up, reached for the button, and held it. I ate some of the bread, drank some of the water, and left the rest on the bench for later.

Then I turned the button over and over, touched it with each of my fingers, and rubbed it on my cheeks and left arm. I felt its smoothness and its concaveness and its roundness and its little holes and its ridge for a long time. After that, I had another bite of bread and some water.

Then I did an incredible thing with my perfect, round, maybe mother-of-pearl button in the silent darkness.

I threw it away.

I flicked the button with my fingers like flipping a coin, except I sort of pushed it away from my body as I flicked it and sent the button into the air, across the room, into the blackness. I heard it hit the floor with a click, and then I heard it roll.

Then I sat on the bench, ate a little more bread, sipped a little more water, and thought about how I would find my button. I thought I could tell from the sound it made where it had landed and which way it had rolled.

I stood and discovered I could walk, so I headed to where I thought the button would be, and then I crawled on my hands and knees and felt the floor, but I could not find it, and then I could not remember where I had begun to look. So I went back to what I thought had been my starting point. I crawled slowly and methodically in an ever-widening spiral, feeling every inch of the floor, and then, after a long time, I found my button, so I returned to the bench and tasted the bread and water. They tasted good. Then I lay down with my button and slept for a long time.

And that was my existence: I ate and drank and flicked my button.

When I woke up again I took a bit of bread and a sip of water. Then I flicked the button, searched for it, and found it. I flicked it so many more times and listened to where it hit and where it rolled that I became an expert. I got so good at finding the button that I could flick it, listen to it hit and roll, walk a few steps, and pick it up.

Then it became too easy, so I would throw the button into a corner so it would hit the wall and bounce, then I would crawl on the floor and feel with my hands until I found it. Sometimes that took a short time, sometimes a long time, but I always found it, and I was always glad to find it. When I found the button, I would reward myself with a little bread and water.

Then I had to make it even more challenging. Sometimes I would throw my button and shout so I wouldn't hear where it hit and wouldn't know where to look based on the noise the button made. Other times I would cover the pail with the blanket, spin until I was dizzy, then throw the button so I wouldn't be sure what direction I had flicked it. But I always found it.

I learned how to eat the bread and drink the water so that right after the last bite and last sip I would have a long sleep with my button next to me, and when I woke up, there would be fresh bread and water.

Then, after hundreds or thousands of flicks, one time I spun around to get dizzy and threw the button as far as I could, like I was throwing a stone, and I shouted so I couldn't hear it hit. Then I crawled and crawled for a long time—a very long time—and still I could not find my button.

After I had searched every inch of the cell at least three times, I began to worry that I would never find the button again, and just then my fingers touched something different, something that was not my button.

It was half a button.

At first I thought I had found a new button, but then I realized that was impossible, so I felt it, and there was a ridge on the half button. I knew it was my button, but it had broken in two.

Actually, it was not half the button. It was less than half. It was like the crescent moon. So I knew there was another piece, a bigger piece with only two holes because I could feel the edges of the holes on the smaller piece. Two of the holes were gone. I sat on the bench and held the small piece. It had a sharp edge and two points, so sharp and pointed that I could cut myself.

I sat on the bench and held the half button for a long time. Then I set my half button on the bench and crawled on the floor until I found the bigger half. I returned to the bench and put the two pieces together; they fit perfectly.

I had some bread and a drink, and I lay down on the bench, covered myself with my blanket, and I was warm, but I did not go to sleep. I thought about what I would do next, and I decided that I would flick both halves of the button at the same time and then I would look for them. I would call the halves Biggy and Smally, and the one that I found first would be the loser, like hide-and-seek. I would want Biggy to win because it would be harder for him to hide because he was bigger than Smally.

Then, while I was making my plans, I felt sleepy.

I knew that more bread and water would come after some sleep, so I decided to wait for the new food and drink before playing the new button game. Maybe it would be like a big tournament, like the World Cup, so I finished the bread and water I had saved, felt good, and fell asleep.

When I woke up the door was open, light was flooding in, and the guard was shouting. "Come on out, kid."

I wrapped myself in my blanket like a chief and

stumbled into the light. The guard stared at me and asked how I was doing. I smiled and said, "I'm great." And then they let me go home to my wife and son.

Anyway, that's how I got through solitary without going crazy—by flicking a button a million times.

I don't have the button now because, before I left the cell, I kicked the two pieces with my big toe into the crack in the corner between the floor and the wall.

MARILEE

MARILEE had never had a date—at least not one where a boy asks you out and you do stuff like dinner and a movie. She'd been to her prom, but she had been fixed up for that. And she'd been fixed up other times by her girlfriends for parties and events they called double dates. She'd been kissed, but she knew what was supposed to happen hadn't happened yet.

And now she was in college—Sturgis College, a real college in Ohio, where most colleges were. The Sturgis campus, like most college campuses, was dotted with old brick buildings that bordered grassy quadrangles intersected by walkways organized like a page in a geometry book, with squares intersected by triangles, with students walking on the triangles and squares, half of them men—in other words, potential dates.

So far Marilee had attended two mixers at the

Commons, but nothing had come of them. Then someone named Oscar DeVilbis called, and a minute later Marilee had a date.

"What do you mean this is your first date?" her roommate Clarisse asked. "You told me about your prom, and what about Cameron? Was that his first or last name? I forget."

"Honest, Clarisse, this is my first real date. Those other things were not dates. They were arranged. The boys were coerced. This boy wants to go out with me of his own free will. He initiated it. It was his idea."

"Okay, relax," said Clarisse. "What's he like?"

"I don't know anything about him," said Marilee. "He called, and I said yes."

"Great," said Clarisse as she pulled the freshman directory from under her pillow. "Here he is."

They sat together on Clarisse's bed. Marilee noticed that Clarisse had made notes next to some of the guys' pictures. "You should try this in your chemistry book," said Marilee.

"Very funny," said Clarisse. Oscar was from Toledo, also in Ohio, and had attended St. Mark's Academy, whatever that was. The tiny picture, about the size of a postage stamp, only showed his face. It was dark with a smile so wide his eyes crinkled. He looked happy. "He could be cute," she said.

"His lips are too thin," said Marilee, but you couldn't really tell that from the tiny smiling photo. Besides, she didn't much care what Oscar looked like. She'd be getting her first date out of the way, and that was all that mattered. She would move on from there.

Marilee considered every boy on campus a possibility, rating them for looks. She was attracted to a couple of guys who appeared to be athletes. She'd followed them to the library and to the gym and wherever else they had headed. Now, that seemed so childish. That was fantasy. This was real. Oscar was real. She wondered about touching—maybe even kissing.

Cameron had kissed her right on the lips, and she had kissed him back. She remembered it vividly, even though it happened three years ago, and it wasn't that good. It was the last thing they did together.

She had told Oscar she would meet him at the Commons, not her dorm, because her side of the room was a mess and would be until parents' weekend.

As she was about to set out, Clarisse said, "Wait. Your glasses." Marilee shook her head. Clarisse lifted Marilee's black-rimmed glasses off the desk and handed them to her. "You bump into things, Marilee. Trust me, wear the glasses." Then Clarisse made Marilee wipe her lipstick off and apply one of Clarisse's shades of pink that you could barely see and looked wet. Then she unbuttoned the top button of Marilee's shirt. "There," said Clarisse. "Good luck." On the way to the Commons a couple of boys eyed her, so she rebuttoned her shirt.

Suddenly, there he was, on the front steps of the Commons, smiling, waiting. Oscar DeVilbis wasn't tall or cute or anything special. She tried to come up with some details to tell Clarisse—some flattering ones. His eyes did crinkle when he smiled, and his teeth were white and straight, but everybody at Sturgis had straight white teeth. His hair was clean and dark, almost silky, and lay naturally in place. The light bounced off it like off a raven's feathers. Oscar's hair was noteworthy.

They strolled across campus to the college theater, his black hair bouncing along the way. She knew hers remained motionless. She tried to stay as close to him as she could without touching him so everyone who saw them would understand they were on a date. He smelled clean. "Want to share a popcorn?" he asked. She did. He paid. She thought they were off to a good start, but after they sat down, before the movie started, Oscar asked, "What's your favorite color?" Marilee didn't have one, but she said, "Blue." Then, after a moment's thought, she added, "What's yours?"

"I don't really have one," he said, "but I like blue too." She decided Oscar DeVilbis might not be that bright. He could be on some kind of athletic scholarship, but she couldn't imagine what sport—certainly not football.

The movie was a French comedy. She was glad she had brought her glasses so she could read the subtitles, but she worried that there would be nudity—or worse. As the movie progressed, she could see it coming. The man and the woman carried a blanket and a basket and picnicked in a beautiful meadow filled with sunshine and Mozart and songbirds. As they lay together on the blanket, Oscar laughed at a couple of inappropriate moments. Then the man removed the girl's top and, for a brief second, her bare breasts filled the screen like twin planets. Marilee stared straight ahead as Oscar exhaled loudly, but they survived the nudity, and then Marilee laughed too.

After the movie they were sitting at a tiny table in a place called the Rathskeller, which was actually upstairs above the campus laundromat, when Oscar leaned close to Marilee's face and said, "I like the glasses. You wore them at the second mixer, but not the first. They make you look sultry."

"You were at both mixers?" *Sultry*, she thought. *Ridiculous.*

"I was too nervous to talk to you, but I saw you, and then I found out who you were. You take art, right?"

"Yup."

He leaned even closer and studied her eyes through her glasses. "I like the color of your eyes. What color are they, exactly?"

"Blue," she said in a stretched-out, two-syllable monotone so it came out, "*ba-loo.*"

"Sorry," he said. "I'm color-blind."

She stared at him. "What?" On the floor below, the dryers spun and the washers sloshed.

"I don't see colors very well."

She reached across the little table and took his hand. "I'm sorry."

He smiled, and his eyes crinkled. "It's okay, Marilee. They say it's not fatal."

She smiled back and gazed into his eyes. She could stroll around campus with him, pointing out the color of things and, maybe, after a while, help him with his clothes. They were still holding hands, although now he was holding hers. *Sultry*, she thought again, and then aloud she said, "I like earth colors, actually—browns and ochres and siennas and mahogany, not really blue at all." She knew she wasn't pretty, but he seemed to think she was. It was good to be thought pretty, even sultry. She tossed her head back so that her hair bounced a little. "So, tell me about yourself."

"Well, I'm from Toledo and, um, I went to St. Mark's. I play the piano."

"Really," she said, leaning forward, her elbows on the table, her chin in her hands. His eyes were a soft, mossy brown, and his lips were not as thin as she had imagined.

MAUREEN AND SYLVIA

GARY Garfield and Fuzzy Mariano were sitting in Fuzzy's basement living room discussing what to do that summer Saturday morning—Fuzzy sprawled on the couch, his feet on the coffee table, and Gary in the Barcalounger, fully reclined, staring at the dingy white ceiling tiles.

There were two weeks left in the summer of 1957 before they would be high school freshmen, no longer boys, almost men. Only two weeks, but it might as well have been a year and a day because Gary and Fuzzy lived life as it came, and two weeks from today was the distant future.

Fuzzy and Gary thought about girls, cars, and sports, but they talked only about cars and sports. Neither had a girlfriend. Neither had even had a date. They were afraid of girls, Gary more so than Fuzzy. That very morning Gary's mother had asked Gary where he was going, and he said to Fuzzy's, and his mother said, out of the blue, "Whatever happened to that cute little O'Reilly girl you used to shoot baskets with?"

Gary had shuddered and said, "Nothing, as far as I know. I gotta go, Mom."

Gary sat up slowly and opened a copy of Popular Mechanics that was sitting on the end table. On the cover was a picture of an ordinary car, except it was in the air, above the houses and trees. The flying car, which the magazine said would be in every driveway by 1967, showed a well-dressed family riding in a sedan with little wings that was flying above a village that looked like Pottville, but a lot nicer.

"So, whatcha wanna do?" asked Fuzzy.

"I dunno," said Gary. "Whatta you wanna do?"

Fuzzy's sixth-grade sister, Mary Anne, strutted through the room with her nose in the air. "Hi, Mary Anne," said Gary. She kept going, ignoring him completely.

Fuzzy had two sisters. The other one, Sylvia, was a senior. Gary was hopelessly in love with her. She was really nice. She always talked to him, but when Gary went to Fuzzy's basement he always hoped she wouldn't be there because, when she was, she asked him questions, and he gave really stupid answers and felt like an idiot. He liked to look at her, but he couldn't talk to her. He didn't know how.

Mary Anne ignored the boys, and they generally ignored her and her superior attitude. When Gary was there, she didn't even talk to Fuzzy. Fuzzy told Gary that

Mary Anne said he was the only one of Fuzzy's friends who was not a retard and the only one who was nice to her, which Gary could not understand because he hardly ever said a word to her, even in school. When he and Mary Anne passed in the hallways, they each looked away as if something on the wall had caught their attention.

Suddenly there was a sound of slamming doors and running—quick, light steps racing down the stairs, and then Gary's heart stopped as Sylvia came twirling into the room wearing a full skirt, bobby socks, loafers, and an incredible pink angora sweater. She threw herself on the couch next to Fuzzy, showing a flash of leg above the knee as she tucked her legs under her. Gary was sitting only three feet away, staring, with only enough sense to close his mouth.

She had a banana in her hand that she started to peel. She was actually going to eat it in front of him. "Hey, stranger," she said to Gary, her voice like a song. "Haven't seen you in a while. You been avoiding me?" and she flashed a smile. Gary said nothing. She peeled another strip. "How's your dad—my favorite teacher? You going to the Fireman's Carnival next week?" That was two questions, or was it three, but even one would have been too many. Gary was speechless. She peeled the last side and started to put the flesh of the banana into her mouth.

"What?" said Gary. She just looked at him, chewing, then swallowing, her tongue darting out to catch white banana bits that stuck to her lips.

"They're gonna have a live band. You dance?" she asked, and then she took another bite.

"Yah," said Gary. "Well, not really." He looked up, and she was staring right at him. She gave him a private smile, raising her eyebrows, clearly for him alone. He had no idea what to do.

Then she jumped up, almost touching him. She was close enough that he could smell her. Her skirt touched his knee. "Well, I got to go take a shower," she said, tossing the uneaten half of her banana to Fuzzy. "Here, stupid, you can finish this," she said as she scampered out of the room.

"I don't want your garbage!" screamed Fuzzy, throwing the banana on the table next to the couch, close enough for Gary to reach. "She is so weird."

"Yeah," said Gary, staring at the banana, wishing he had the strength to reach over and taste where her mouth had just been, but he knew he didn't.

"So, whatta you want to do?" asked Fuzzy.

Gary didn't know. "I wish I had five hundred dollars," he said, relieved to be able to think and talk again.

"How come?"

"This ad is in every month," said Gary, who had been thumbing backward through the magazine with the flying car on the cover. "You can buy these war surplus Army jeeps. They come in a crate, and you just put them together."

"We could go in on one," said Fuzzy.

They got pencil and paper and figured that in maybe

two years Gary could raise his half, if he got a summer job. Gary examined their math. It was true. They could do it, and even though they both knew it wouldn't happen, it felt good to know that, someday, they would be old enough to raise enough money to own a car.

Without agreeing on a plan, they headed downtown together, past the school and the Episcopal church, the Methodist church, and the Presbyterian church, cut through the weeds behind the Regal Theater toward Beckman's where they entered without a word, sat at the counter, and ordered a vanilla phosphate and a cherry Coke. "The usual," said Beckman.

Beckman, like most adults, was hopelessly out-of-date, out of touch, and funny looking. He had a little tuft of hair that Fuzzy said looked like he had skinned a mouse and glued it to his head. Below the dead mouse was an inch of freckled skin, then an inch-wide line of white hair around the back of his head that ended just above each ear. He wore old-lady glasses that slid down his pointed nose, and he always wore the same coat sweater that was covered with pills. All that made him look old, but he wasn't stooped or wrinkled, and his voice wasn't old, so maybe he wasn't really that old. Gary couldn't decide if Beckman was a nice guy or not.

After making their drinks, Beckman took their dimes. As they left, headed somewhere or other, two girls on bicycles pulled up, blocking their path. Angela Courtney was in most of Gary's classes. She was the smartest girl in school, and she and Gary competed for the highest marks. When he decided to ask a girl out, Gary intended to ask Angela, and he assumed she would say yes. With her was Maureen O'Reilly, who was a year younger than Angela.

The girls straddled the frames of their bikes and leaned on the handlebars. They all just looked at each other. "Hi, Fuzzy," said Angela, breaking the silence.

"Hi, Angela," said Gary. The boys put their hands in their pants pockets. Fuzzy said nothing. Maureen smiled.

"Whatcha guys doin'?" asked Angela.

"Nothin'," said Fuzzy. "What're you guys doin'?"

"Nothin'," said Angela. They looked at each other some more and smiled, then Angela said, "Well, gotta go," and she and Maureen rode off. They could hear the girls screeching and giggling as they turned the corner onto Elm Street.

The next day Gary arrived and headed down to Fuzzy's basement. Mary Anne said, "Upstairs." Gary just stared at her. She pointed up and nodded.

He trudged up the stairs. Fuzzy could not be upstairs during the day because the Marianos never used their regular kitchen or regular upstairs living room or dining room except for Sunday dinner, holidays, and confirmations.

When Gary told his parents the Marianos lived in their basement, his mother had said, "That's ridiculous. You shouldn't say things like that. I've been in their house. It's very nice."

"Of course it's nice, Mom. But they never use it."

He could tell she didn't believe him, but it was true. In Gary's basement they just stored stuff that they would eventually throw out. Gary's father did have a workshop with a few power tools, but he hardly ever went down there. But the Marianos' basement featured a full kitchen and living room (not a game room—a real living room) with couches, carpeting, and floor lamps that looked the same as their upstairs living room, except the basement had a more lived-in look because, well, they lived in it.

Gary stood in the archway between the front hallway and stared in disbelief. There were people in the Marianos' upstairs in broad daylight. There, in front of him, in the unused, impeccably clean living room on the clear plastic-covered couch sat Fuzzy and Angela, looking as if they belonged there. Fuzzy had one arm resting on the back of the couch behind Angela's shoulders. The two were mere inches apart. "Hey, Gary," said Fuzzy.

"Hey, Gary," said Angela.

Gary said nothing. They acted so casual, as if this were nothing, sitting alone together on the upstairs couch in the pristine living room. There were two Cokes on the coffee table, making round puddles on the glass top. Fuzzy's mother would kill him. At that moment Gary smelled something in the never-used kitchen, and Mrs. Mariano appeared in the living room with a plate of cookies that she set in front of Angela. "Fresh from the oven," she said. Then she pinched Fuzzy's cheek and said sweetly, "Oh, hello, Gary," but she did not offer him a cookie. Then she disappeared. Fuzzy took a swig of his Coke and wiped his mouth with his hand. He didn't invite Gary to come into the room. Fuzzy turned to Angela and said, "Like I was saying, I'm really looking forward to college, then maybe business school. This town is changing. The world is changing." Then he turned to Gary and said, "You want to do something later? I'll call you." Then he turned back to Angela.

Gary backed out of the room and headed out the back door.

What was all this stuff about college? Fuzzy going to college? He couldn't even pass eighth grade algebra. And the way Angela was sitting there, right next to him, and the way she was looking at him, at Fuzzy. They hadn't even started high school. Life was going by too fast. And, as far as he could see, the world was not changing, except maybe for flying cars and stuff like that. He walked down the street, shuffling along the gutter, kicking a stone forward a few feet and then kicking it again.

He didn't want to go home. There was nothing to do. He headed in another direction, down Maple Street, Angela's street, past her house, then three doors down past Maureen's house. The O'Reillys had a huge porch. Maureen's head popped up, and she waved. Gary didn't wave back.

He shuffled to the park, sat on a swing, but didn't swing, then turned around and trudged past Maureen's house again. Maureen was still sitting there, but this time she didn't wave. She was probably reading. He knew she was an avid reader, and he could only see the top of her head. He kept moving until he passed Angela's again. He wondered how long she would stay at Fuzzy's. Then he made his way to the Catholic church corner and back again, toward home. When he reached Maureen's he turned, casually stuffed his hands into his pockets, and plodded up her front walk. "Hi," he said.

She sat up and seemed surprised. "Hi, Gary."

"Um," he said. "Well, I was just heading down to Beckman's for a phosphate. You wanna come?"

"Sure," she said. "Why not?" She stood and threw her book on the swing. She was taller than she looked on her bike, but a little shorter than he was. She was wearing shorts that showed off her tanned legs. She used to be short and stocky and sloppy with bruises all over. She brushed some fine, clean, red hair away from her face and revealed the freckles that dotted her pug nose. It seemed like only her nose was the same from when they used to shoot baskets during her tomboy phase. "Where's Fuzzy?" she asked.

"I dunno."

They walked by the apartments where the "gypsies" lived. That's what some people called them but, of course, they weren't gypsies, just poor people. Beckman owned those ramshackle apartments, and the town fathers were always after him to keep them repaired or, at least, cleaned up, but he never did. Then they cut behind the Baptist church, past the "graveyard" where abandoned railroad cars had been rusting for years, then past the paper mill and the noxious odors from its vats of toxic chemicals that boiled day and night, endlessly breaking down old magazines, newsprint, and rags into pungent slurry. Some people complained about the smell that drifted over the town, but for Gary, it would not be Pottville without it. They emerged into downtown on Main Street from behind Bank-em-Easy's Cigar Store where you could place bets on horse races—and just about anything else.

They strolled in silence all the way to Beckman's. Maureen didn't ask any questions, like why he had just passed her house three times when he said he was going to Beckman's, or why on earth he decided to talk to her for the first time in a long time when she always smiled at him in school, but he always ignored her. The silence didn't seem to bother Maureen at all.

Beckman came over and was all smiles. "Well, well, well," he said, and he wouldn't take any money for Maureen's cherry Coke, but he did allow Gary to pay for his vanilla phosphate.

As they left Beckman's and headed down Main Street, Maureen said, "He's so nice, but he has that funny hair."

He told her what Fuzzy had said about the skinned mouse, except he didn't say that Fuzzy was the one who said it, and she laughed and laughed. "Oh, Gary, that's terrible." And they stared at each other.

"Sorry," he said.

"Sure you are," she said, still smiling.

They walked a block to Bemis's Appliances (the blind man's shop), which not only sold used appliances but records too. By some magical power, although blind, Mr. Bemis knew where every appliance and every record was located.

The first time Gary bought a record from Mr. Bemis he showed it to his mother, and she asked him if he'd gone to the blind man's shop. He said no, to Bemis's, and she laughed. Gary couldn't believe it when she told him Mr. Bemis was blind. She said it was even more incredible because he had lost his sight as a child and had to learn to be blind; he had to train his other senses. Mr. Bemis was pretty amazing. Fuzzy always asked Mr. Bemis for three or four records just to see him pull them out ten times faster than a sighted person could.

As they entered the shop Mr. Bemis said, "Hello, Gary, and who's the young lady?"

"It's me, Mr. Bemis, Maureen."

"Ah," said Mr. Bemis, as if a princess had entered his store. "I got Elvis. You want to hear it?"

He moved his fingers lightly down the shelf and pulled out an LP. He had hundreds, maybe thousands of records—used records—mostly LPs that he sometimes sold for a dollar, sometimes two—never more than five.

If you asked Mr. Bemis how he knew who you were before you spoke, he said he smelled you, but it was more than that. No one ever stole from Mr. Bemis, even though it would have been easy—easier than stealing magazines from Beckman who was always alert. Beckman had mirrors all over his store, curved like birdbath globes, and he told the young kids to keep away from the magazines.

Kids stole candy from Beckman too because kids were trickier than Beckman and worked together in teams.

After they listened to a few Elvis songs that, for some reason, Maureen swooned over (Gary thought Elvis sounded like a hillbilly), Gary accompanied her back to her house. As he left her at the end of her front sidewalk she said, "I'll be home tonight." Gary said nothing.

He ate everything his mother served for dinner that night and asked for more. After dinner, he took a bath and used some of his dad's Old Spice, then washed most of it off. His mom said, "Don't you look nice."

"So, what's up?" asked his dad.

"Nothing," said Gary, moving toward the door.

"Where you off to?" asked his mom.

"Nowhere," he said, and he headed toward Fuzzy's. But once around the corner, he turned toward Maureen's.

She was wearing a blue skirt and pink lipstick. They strolled around town for two hours and didn't say much. By then it was nearly dark, but the light in Schlumberger's showroom stayed on until ten. They stopped and looked at the new 1957 Studebaker Silver Hawk, and he told her about the new invention called directional signals and the supercharged 289 engine that could blow away the DeSoto. "Really, Gary?" she said, impressed. When they past the paper mill, Maureen said, "You know, for some reason, I love that smell. It smells like old books."

"Me too," he said. When they were under the oaks on Sycamore Street, she leaned against him, and then they turned the corner and, under the sycamores on Oak

Street, he reached down and took her hand in his. They held hands until it was dark, and the stars and the fireflies came out. They sat for a few minutes on her front porch. "You know, Maureen, it's hard to believe, but next year I'll be in high school. This town is changing. The world is changing."

"Really, Gary?"

MORGAN THE PLUMBER

Reprint from NDQ – North Dakota Quarterly
Volume 77, Number 4, p. 38
Fall 2012
Nominated for a Pushcart Prize

I'M not really a writer, but it's what I've always wanted to be, so I decided to go to what is called a writers' workshop. This one was held at McLean University in Ohio in a little town called Westerville where the only stores besides the grocery are the feed store and two gas stations. The feed store sells everything: clothes, hardware, pots and pans, you name it. It's an old-fashioned town, but the college is modern—plenty of concrete and glass and flat roofs. There were ten of us in the workshop, including eight women.

The only other male, a retired postal worker from Des Moines, Iowa, named Cosgrove Cobb, was about my age.

On the first day of class our teacher, a writer named Hoskins Pillford, introduced himself, looked up at us from the head of the conference table, and said, "Nature." We all looked back at him with blank expressions, and he continued: "Write. Write something about nature. *Now.* Write for ten minutes." So we did. I don't remember what I wrote—something about trees, I think. I destroyed it as soon as I had the chance.

For the entire ten minutes Cosgrove wrote with ferocity, bearing down so hard at one point that he broke his pencil. He had a spare. In fact, he had plenty of pencils, all of which said "Property of US Postal Service." He was left-handed and wrote sort of upside down, the paper almost sideways, his hand above his handwriting, his tongue darting in and out.

Hoskins asked for volunteers to read what they had written. I looked down, putting my hands under the table. Cosgrove raised his hand, and this is the amazing thing that he read:

> One crisp morning Morgan the Plumber, his wife, Meg, and his dog, Moppy, were strolling in the pasture. As the wind blew the mist from the waves of grass, Moppy tried to bite his own doggy breath. Morgan stood in the open field, waving his arms. He felt nothing, but he knew the air was heavy with the unseen. He knew this air had slowly

formed this field, turned mountain into beach, fish to rock, sculpted the hills, made the river, and made the grasses weave. Morgan the Plumber knew there is no evil. There is only beauty.

Hoskins seemed stunned. No one spoke for a full minute. "I'm finished," said Cosgrove. "That's all I wrote. Is it too short?"

"It's fine. In fact, it's very good," said Hoskins. "Now, tell me, Cosgrove. Who is Morgan the Plumber?"

"He's my character," said Cosgrove. "He's in all my stories."

"I see," said Hoskins. "Tell me about the dog, Moppy." Cosgrove didn't know what breed of dog Moppy was or even what color it was or whether the dog was male or female. "Does the dog look like a mop?" asked Hoskins.

"No," said Cosgrove. "It has short hair. Look. It's not important what Moppy looks like. It's what he is."

"Or she," said Hoskins.

"Whatever," said Cosgrove.

"Now," said Hoskins, "who else would like to read?" Three women raised their hands. Cosgrove had broken the ice, and the workshop was underway.

Cosgrove and I—and Hoskins too, as it turned out— were staying at a campus inn called the McLean Arms. Cosgrove and I bonded; the women bonded with each other and with Hoskins. Truthfully, I think the women intimidated me. I know they intimidated Cosgrove. I stayed at the inn because I was too old to stay in the bathroom-down-the-hall dorm like the other would-be writers.

The campus bar, The Rathskeller, happened to be right there at the inn. The first night, after I'd written my "short piece of fiction" for the next day, I went down to the Rathskeller, which wasn't in the cellar at all; it was right off the lobby. Cosgrove was there, and we sat at a table and had a beer. We talked about our kids and our retirement and how young all the college kids looked— they seemed more like high school or junior high kids to us. Cosgrove said he'd never shown his writing to anyone before, and I said. "Well, I'm glad you did," He said nothing more, so I said, "Aren't you glad you did?"

"I don't know," he said, looking at his beer bottle. "Maybe."

Most of the times when Cosgrove and I were in the bar, Hoskins was there too, sitting on a stool and staring at a pair of ice cubes floating in scotch whiskey.

Hoskins Pillford was a real writer, a published novelist. I called him "What's the Story" Pillford because he would ask the class at least twice every day, "What is the story?" That's the way he taught. He would ask questions, but there were never any right answers. When you offered an answer, he would challenge it with another question. It's called the Socratic method, and it was frustrating because I had decided that the best way to search for answers was to write fiction. But Hoskins seemed to think that what you needed for fiction were questions, not answers.

Don't get me wrong about Hoskins. He was a good teacher—the best teacher I've ever had. He inspired me. But he did seem to be in a quandary.

Hoskins was handsome in a loose-jointed, disheveled sort of way with long hair and arms and fingers that all flopped around as he strode around the room and lectured. I guessed he was about fifty, but he could've been sixty. His age notwithstanding, the women were entranced, and he knew it. He wore baggy pants and shirts and looked as if he had lost weight, which he had. He insisted on a break every hour, and we soon discovered that he smoked a cigarette during each one.

Every day Hoskins wrote a single word on the blackboard. He said it was to get us going. We didn't have to use it, but if we couldn't think of anything to write, we were to use that word and go from there.

The sessions ended at three p.m., and every night we were expected to write a piece of short fiction and bring it to class the next day. I found out that "a piece of short fiction" meant a story.

On the second day, Tuesday, the word *art* was the cue word, and Cosgrove had a long story ready that started, "Morgan the Plumber liked art." As the story continued, Morgan went for walks with Meg and Moppy on the beach, searching for stones or rocks the size of a baseball or smaller, stones you could hold in your hand. He would take them back home and paint them. Morgan had to find rocks that had a certain shape—rocks that told a story. Most of his time was spent finding the right rock.

The painting was more or less incidental, just so other people could see what was in the rock. A rock could be some kind of animal, a tiger, an automobile, or even two people kissing. The shape was the thing.

But Cosgrove's story wasn't about the rocks. It's hard to say what it was about.

It was clear Morgan loved his wife, Meg, but he seemed to suspect she was guilty of infidelity, although there was no indication that she had been unfaithful; in fact, she seemed firmly devoted to Morgan. Still, he watched her suspiciously. When she talked to other men, it upset him. He didn't like her to wear clothes that he considered "enticing."

One day a call came in requesting help for a plumbing emergency, but Morgan refused to go. "Tell them I'm busy," he said. "Why can't people fix their own toilets is what I'd like to know."

In another unconnected scene, he refused to go to church with Meg because the minister preached that pride was a sin.

"Nonsense," said Morgan, "all you got to do is look at the animals, the turkey struttin' around. Them girl turkeys eat it up."

Hoskins asked him, "What does the rock painting have to do with your story?"

Cosgrove thought for a moment before he said, "Well, that doesn't matter, does it? That's just what Morgan does. That's what he is. He's not really all connected himself."

But the more I think about it, it sort of felt like part of the story. It just did, but I didn't see it at first. I'm not sure I even knew what the connection was. It's hard to articulate, but it was there. Morgan said the rocks had souls before they were painted and after they were painted. With all his quirks and idiosyncrasies, there was something about Morgan the Plumber. I saw some of myself in Morgan's exaggerated faults.

On the third morning, Wednesday, a pretty young lady joined our seminar. She sat next to Hoskins at the head of the table. She didn't contribute anything. She just observed. When he went out for his cigarette breaks, she accompanied him. We all knew that Hoskins was married because it was in his bio the school had sent us when we signed up for the workshop:

> This year's fiction section will be taught by acclaimed novelist Hoskins Pillford, author of *In the Gloaming, The Afterglow,* and *Candles for Elvira.* Hoskins is head of the creative writing program at Ohio State University and lives in Columbus with his wife, Miriam, and their three teenage daughters.

That pretty young lady was certainly not the mother of three teenage girls. She could be a teenager herself. And she called him Hoskins.

Hoskins was on a special diet he called "the water diet," so he had to drink a quart of water during our session every day. There was always a plastic quart bottle of water in front of him on the table, and he did work at drinking the whole thing. He had lost twenty pounds in the last three months, he said, and had ten more to go. At one point the girl found him a paper cup and kept refilling it to make sure he drank it. "Drink your water," she said softly many times that session. The word for that day was *science*. Here is Cosgrove's story:

> Morgan the Plumber liked science. He learned that light is something that moves—that it moves very fast, but not that fast, not infinitely fast.
>
> For example, light took years to reach Earth from the stars. That fact puzzled Morgan. It was a concept he could not grasp, at least not until the night of the plumbers' union Christmas party.
>
> Morgan rented a tuxedo and a pleated shirt. Meg wore a silver sequined dress. She sparkled, and the eyes of many plumbers were upon her.
>
> Across the room he saw her laughing and talking with Jack, his young apprentice. She gazed up at Morgan. They exchanged glances. He saw again the lovelight in her eyes.
>
> *Yet*, he thought, *does she love me now?* as he suddenly realized that the waves from that lovelight had left her eye some time ago.

When he finished reading he said, "I tried to make it all connect this time, so it had to be short. I had to leave Moppy out."

"Good job," said Hoskins.

I went down to the bar early that night just to talk to Cosgrove about the young girl. He was late. I had downed one beer and was about to give up and go to bed when he finally showed up. "So," I said as soon as he sat down with his beer, "what did you think of Hoskins' little girlfriend?"

"Jim," he said, "I've been sitting in the library since three o'clock, and I've written nothing for tomorrow. He told me I had to get away from Morgan, but I can't. All I can write about is Morgan the Plumber. I know Hoskins is right. I don't know anything about plumbing, so it looks like Morgan doesn't know anything about plumbing. The only tool he has is a pipe wrench. It's the only plumber's tool I know. And he's such a jerk. His wife loves him, yet he treats her like crap. He's jealous. He's angry. He hates his work."

I tried to calm him down. I suggested that Morgan didn't have to be a plumber. He could be a farmer or anything. "I don't know anything about farming or anything else. All I know is postal work, but who wants to read about a postal worker sorting mail? Whoop-de-doo. Some story."

I felt sorry for Cosgrove. Everyone would be disappointed if he didn't show up the next day with a story. Morgan the Plumber was the hit of the class. Cosgrove and I talked for a long time. I ended up having three beers, and he had two. The whole time Hoskins was sitting at the bar staring at his scotch. He looked like he was in a bad mood.

The next day, Thursday, the young girl wasn't there, so the other women hovered around Hoskins during his cigarette breaks. Cosgrove and I kept our distance. A couple of times Hoskins glanced at us and displayed a weary, knowing smile.

After our lunch break, Hoskins asked Cosgrove to read again. When Cosgrove said he didn't have a story, Hoskins said, "You need to write something for tomorrow, Cosgrove. Anything. Please try."

"Can it be about Morgan?"

Hoskins sighed. "I'd prefer not, but yes, Cosgrove, it can be about Morgan." Then he ran his long fingers through his hair, picked up his water bottle, and took a long drink. "God," he said, "I hate water."

The young girl had, as I said, first showed up on Wednesday and stayed all day, but she didn't show up at all on Thursday. On Friday she wasn't there either until, right after the last cigarette break, she slipped into the room and sat next to Hoskins.

Hoskins ignored her. He asked Cosgrove if he had managed to write a story, and Cosgrove said he had. It was called "Yesterday Afternoon." This is what he read:

> "You know," Morgan the Plumber said at the dinner table, "yesterday afternoon I watched a Cinemascope movie on TV. To fit the whole picture in they just squashed it sideways. So the grand piano

was short and fat. The people all looked skinny, elegant, with long, pointy fingers, taking long, graceful strides. Everything was unreal. But after I watched for a while, it all seemed normal."

"So what was it about?" asked Meg. "Maybe I've seen it."

"I doubt it," he said. "There was this really mean guy, rich and powerful. Everyone hated him, but you could tell they envied him too. The part I saw was in his office, which had a huge desk, a piano, living room furniture, a bedroom, a bathroom, and a table set with china and crystal. There was a fight, and they broke all the china."

Morgan leaped up from the table, exchanging imaginary punches with himself, slashing the air, staggering around the dining room. Then, stand-ing behind his chair, a little out of breath from the fight, he said, "So they're still in the office, and the guy in the movie gave this blonde girl a short fur coat, and she went into the bedroom to try it on, then came back naked, except for the coat," and then Morgan strutted around like a girl showing off a fur coat and pretended to fluff his hair like a woman. Then he said, "Just then this guy's wife and little girl walk in." And Morgan made a face like the little girl did in the movie, his knees bent together, his eyes wide, his mouth in an "O" and two fingers over the "O."

"Let's pause there," said Hoskins, interrupting. "Very good, Cosgrove, but before we go on, I want to make two points. First, this is an excellent example of what is called a 'frame story,' which means it's a story within a story; in this case, it's a story that Morgan the Plumber is telling to his wife. Secondly, this is a breakthrough for Cosgrove because he has escaped Morgan the Plumber and introduced new characters."

At that moment the pretty girl turned to Hoskins and asked if he would like some water. Hoskins didn't respond. "You're not drinking your water like you're supposed to," she said as he continued to ignore her.

"Please read on, Cosgrove," said Hoskins, but before Cosgrove could read a word the girl stood, slowly picked up the half full quart bottle, and poured the water over Hoskins' head. The water ran over his face, soaked his shirt front, and ran into his lap. He sat motionless. Then she bounced the empty bottle on the table and walked out. Two of the women hurried to the ladies room and brought back some paper towels. Hoskins wiped off the table and then himself before dismissing us for the day.

That night, Friday night, the night before the last day of our seminar, Hoskins was at the bar as usual. I heard his gruff voice and glanced up to see him stuffing his cell phone into his jacket pocket. Then he caught my eye, slipped down off his stool, and shuffled over to our table.

Cosgrove and I looked at each other. "Sit down. Join us," I said. Cosgrove smiled and nodded. Hoskins gave the bartender a signal, a little circle in the air with his index finger, and sat down.

Hoskins immediately turned on Cosgrove. "Your story pissed me off." Cosgrove looked up, bewildered. Hoskins smiled. "Because, apparently, it's about me." He laughed, and we laughed. He studied both of us for a minute. "You're both retired, right?" We nodded. "You don't know what to do with yourselves, so you're going to be writers." He turned to Cosgrove. "You're good."

"How about me?"

"I think you could be," he said, and then he saw my expression. "Look," he said, "I can't tell a good writer from a bad writer. Anyway, you have potential. That's a good thing to have, right? But you're overeducated, so you over-write. You need to let it loose. Let it flow. Stop squeezing it out. Anyway, we write because we want to write, not because we are good or bad."

"So," I said, pointing a finger at him, "just what is a story?" I know there was a little anger in my voice. "And I don't want another question this time. I want an answer."

The bartender set a scotch on the rocks in front of Hoskins and brought us two beers. "On me," said Hoskins. Then he put his hand on my sleeve and spoke softly. "Jim, my friend, there is one story. There are a million stories. There are no stories." He moved his hand over the table as if calming the waters. He took a strong sip, shivered, and sat back. He glanced first at Cosgrove and then at me. "If you let it loose and let your creative juices flow, the reader will make a story out of it. It's the reader who tells the story. That's your answer. Now, let's talk about something else."

So we did.

Hoskins took another strong sip, shivered again, and wiped his mouth with his hand in what, for him, was an elegant gesture. "That girl who came to class," said Hoskins, "the water girl—her name is Heather. She's my student at Ohio State. She followed me here...somehow. What am I going to do? I don't want to hurt her. After that first day I told her to come to my room. I told her we'd just talk, but I knew what would happen. I know the flesh is weak. So then I changed my mind and told her not to come, to go back home where she belonged." He took another swallow. "You know why I changed my mind? Because every night I watch you two guys sitting here at this table. I know you guys have wives and families. I can tell just by looking at you. I knew what you thought of me."

Hoskins went back to his scotch. As Cosgrove and I were heading for the elevator, Cosgrove was shaking his head as he said, "Hoskins didn't understand my story."

"Oh, I think he got it."

"No, it needs work."

Saturday was the last day of the workshop, and Hoskins arrived with a fresh quart of water and a fresh woman. She was younger than Hoskins, but a lot older than the other woman. She could easily have teenage daughters. He introduced her to us as his wife, Miriam. She had driven up from Columbus, and when the conference ended, they were going to Gambier to meet some friends and enjoy a brief romantic interlude away from the kids. "She'll be my bodyguard today," he said. We all laughed, except Miriam, who only smiled a little.

With Hoskin's wife there, the arrangement around the table had reversed itself with the older women sitting closer to Hoskins. He asked Cosgrove to finish reading his story. "I think everyone remembers where we left off." We nodded.

> "Then," said Morgan, "his wife walked out on him. After that, everybody walked out on him—his partner, his best friend, and a woman who might have been his sister; I'm not sure. She told him his father was so ashamed he had moved to another city and was living under an assumed name." There was a catch in Morgan's voice. He bowed his head. "Meg, the ending was so tragic."

> "But he was such a bad man."

> Morgan peered up at her and said, "No, Meg, no. That's not it."

> "You said he was mean."

> "He wasn't a nice man, but that's not what the movie was about." Again, Morgan stood and held

out his arms. "This man was fully alive—fighting." Morgan held up his fists. "Don't you see, Meg?"

"I'm trying, Morgan."

"Look at the stars, Meg," he said, staring at the ceiling, his hands pointing skyward. "They stretch out in all directions, forever. We're just a little accident in the middle of nothing. We're hungry. We have desires, emotions. That's all. You need to see that."

"What I see, Morgan, is that your veal cutlet is getting cold." Meg stood and led him to the table. "Sit down. Eat. Drink your water." He sat. She bent and touched his ear with her lips. "I'll never leave you, Morgan," she whispered. He lifted his glass up.

Near the end of the reading, I put my pencil down and just listened. Cosgrove stopped and made eye contact with everyone. He was finished.

Hoskins stood and placed his fists on the table. "Well, what did we all think?"

"I really liked it," said one of the women who, it turned out, was named Margaret. "This time it was about Meg."

"Very good," said Hoskins, and then he turned to me. "Jim, what did you think? You seemed entranced."

"Well," I said, "I would have just said, at the end

there, 'He lifted his glass,' instead of 'He lifted his glass up.'"

"Very good," said Hoskins, "much better rhythm. What else?"

"It's a small thing, but I would have used roast beef instead of veal cutlet. Morgan is a roast beef kind of guy, and so am I." Everyone laughed.

"Is that all, Jim?" asked Hoskins.

"No," I said. Then I stopped, at a loss for words. The day before I had read a story that Hoskins had said was "clever" about a couple who tried to train a dog, but the dog ended up training them. There was nothing in it about desire and not that much emotion, either. Hoskins leaned toward me, pressing in. "There's more, Jim?"

I shrugged, smiled, and said, "Well, Hoskins, for one thing, it looks like you're off the hook."

Hoskins laughed.

"And I'm on it?" I said.

The woman named Margaret said, "What's going on here?"

Everyone's eyes turned to Hoskins. "You tell her, Jim," he said. "What's going on here?"

Then all eyes turned to me. "Well," I said, "Hoskins said to me last night that he thought this story was about him, but now, you see, it isn't."

"What's going on with you, Jim?" said Margaret, "You're just sitting there. You stopped writing down everything everyone says."

The ten of us had spent the week searching for what

the story is. The women were all staring at me. I said, "Last year we went to Paris and saw Notre Dame, and I finally understood what a Gothic cathedral is. It's more like a feeling."

"And that's what the story did to you, Jim?" asked Hoskins rhetorically. I glanced down at my mechanical pencil lying quietly on the table. Margaret smiled.

"There," said Hoskins, "that's that. Well put, Jim. Now I think this might be a good place to end." It was early, but the seminar was over. To go on would have been an anticlimax.

We all stood outside the concrete and glass building in the sun, said our goodbyes, and slowly dispersed. Cosgrove and I chatted for a few minutes with Hoskins and Miriam. Miriam was really nice. I liked them together. We all talked about our kids.

Standing next to our cars in the hotel parking lot, shaking hands goodbye the way men do, Cosgrove handed me an unsharpened "Property of US Postal Service" pencil. We promised to keep in touch, although I knew we would not. "You were right about the veal cutlet," he said. "It should have been roast beef."

WOMEN ARE HARD TO FIGURE

IT'S difficult to say this without sounding like I'm bragging, but as with many great lovers, I started early. My first conquest transpired in the summer of 1954. I was a mere thirteen years old.

One of my fondest memories of those summer days was doing nothing. One such time was a Saturday in June; school was not out for the summer yet, and I was sitting in the park behind the bandstand with Tommy Burns and Tony Angelo. We were just sitting in the grass, doing nothing, with the vigor that thirteen-year-old boys apply to that most pleasurable of activities. The three of us had spent all day together traipsing around the village, talking, wrestling, laughing. We had no money, no plans, no ideas. We had nothing, and we matched that by doing nothing.

Anyway, Tommy and Tony were resting there in the

grass, eyeing the clouds as they drifted, excitedly interrupting each other, telling me how the Saturday before
they had seen Robert Cosgrove at the movies with Jo
Ellen Curtis. Tommy and Tony had been sitting three
rows behind them. They agreed that Robert had slipped
his arm around her and was kissing her, but there was
violent debate as to whether he was "feeling her up." I
was just listening. I had not been there. I had no idea
what "feeling her up" was, nor was I much enlightened
by their discussion that consisted of "He was not," "Was
so," "Was not," and so forth. "Feeling up" sounded a little rough, but I knew about kissing and that, by itself,
was exciting enough for me.

Robert Cosgrove was a big kid, older, but only by a
year. I surveyed the sky and thought about kissing, and
maybe that day, right at that moment, was the first time
the idea of kissing a girl appealed to me. In fact, just
lying there in the grass and thinking about it made me
feel good, different. And then, for some reason, a picture
of Irene Russo floated into the air between me and the
clouds. Irene.

I didn't hear Tommy and Tony anymore. I was in deep
contemplation. How could I kiss a girl? Where? Who? I
needed a date. I needed to take a girl to the movies.

I carefully considered all the girls in my class but, of
course, I settled on Irene Russo. She had red hair and
didn't talk much. She was not one of the really knockout
cute girls, but she was pretty. Her smile was slight, her

nose turned up a little, and although I had never touched her, she looked soft.

I was smart in math. Once, Irene had come over to the boys' table in the cafeteria and asked me for help with her math homework. I remember she smelled clean, like soap. She was wearing a mint green angora cardigan— always worn backward—which I found particularly enticing. Her father drove a Chrysler with a semiautomatic transmission. It was black and always showroom shiny. For some reason, that was a crucial point in her favor.

But other than that one day in the cafeteria, I had never talked to Irene except to say, "Hi."

For the record, here is a complete transcript of all our previous conversations (except for that one day in the cafeteria):

Irene Russo: "Hi."

Me: "Hi."

Since boys were afraid to talk to girls, and any girl who talked to a boy was in danger of being considered "forward," dating preliminaries had to be carried out by third parties. I decided not to involve Tony or Tommy because they would screw it up. This was a delicate operation. So, after some serious reflection, I decided the first step was for my best friend Chester to ask his cousin Susie if Irene Russo "liked" me. I need to explain here what "liking" means. "Liking" was a term of art; it meant something specific, something big, something ineffable. If you saw a gaggle of girls talking and one said, "Guess what? Jeannie likes Billie," there would be pandemonium, screaming, jumping and "Oh, my God!" for several minutes before things calmed down. It was a big thing to "like" someone; it was a major emotional commitment.

"Liking" was not necessarily exclusive. (The term for exclusiveness was "going steady.") Cute girls had a lot of boys who "liked" them, but many of the girls had none. The same held true for the boys. You had to be careful not to set your sights too high, or you could be crushed. And such a rejection, even through third parties, even though invariably couched in the euphemism, "She thinks you have a nice personality," was devastating. But with the impossible dream of a kiss in the balance, I was willing to risk it.

The roundabout intelligence gathering required to discover if Irene "liked" me took longer than I had anticipated. After a few days, the strain of the delay began to show. At dinner one evening my mother glanced at me, her eyebrows squished together, and inquired, "Peter, is something wrong at school? Is that Farini boy bothering you again?"

"No, no Mom, it's fine. I'm fine. Everything is fine. He doesn't bother me anymore. I took care of that. Everything is fine." I gave her my best relaxed smile to sell it.

"Yeah, sure, Peter," said my sister. She tilted her head slightly and grinned at me. Although a year older than I, she may have been aware of the Byzantine intelligence operation Chester and I had unleashed.

My dad looked up from his meat loaf and mashed potatoes, surveying each of us briefly. He was still wearing his white shirt and tie from the office, the tie slightly loosened, and the top button of his shirt undone. He reached over and ruffled my hair. "Leave him alone, Helen," he said. "He's fine—apparently."

Finally, after almost a week of worry, I was rewarded for my prudent selection.

Irene "liked" me.

It is hard to exaggerate the euphoria, the emotional lift it gave me to learn that Irene Russo had succumbed to my charms. All that remained was for me to swoop in and collect the prize.

Next came Phase Two, which was to ask for a date. I quickly ruled out asking Irene directly, person-to-person. I simply didn't have the nerve. The transaction would have to be conducted by phone. Initially, I considered making the call myself, but upon further review I realized I had absolutely no idea how to go about it. I would call her. She would answer the phone—but then what? I had no idea, so I decided to remain in the background a little longer.

My bold plan was to have Chester call Irene and propose a date. We made the call together from my parents' bedroom where the extension was located, out of earshot of my mother, and worse, my sister. Chester and I seated ourselves on the edge of the double bed and stared at the phone: a black, dial-less, pushbutton-less communication device that rested on the bedside table.

My hands covered my face. My breathing was audible and visible, but Chester seemed relaxed as he lifted the receiver to make the call that could set my first sexual conquest in motion.

Chester calmly told the operator, "Ludlow 6-0478," as if this was just an ordinary phone call. There was a pause, and then he continued: "Hello, Mrs. Russo. Is Irene there?" Chester put his hand over the mouthpiece of the handset, stuffed it against my mother's pillow, and whispered excitedly, "She's there!" Then he cradled the handset against his ear again and waited. Suddenly, he blurted, "Hey, Irene, would you like to go to the movies with Pete?" He paused. "It's me, Chester." He shoved the handset into the pillow again and whispered, "She said okay!" He hung up the phone.

Chester and I beamed at each other in triumph. Then we fell back onto the bed and started pummeling each other before we sprinted down the stairs, through the house, and into the yard where we rolled on the lawn, pummeling each other again.

My first date was set. It was not necessary to establish time or place. There was only one theater, The Rialto, and one Saturday matinee.

"The Date" was big news all over school the next day. I received plenty of congratulations and envious looks for my fast-moving ways with women. I was even told that a couple of other girls "liked" me. My success with Irene had created a bandwagon effect.

I let it be known that I would meet Irene inside the theater. There were many reasons for that strategy. There was the financial aspect, of course, although that was not paramount. Still, I literally had to count my pennies because my allowance was only a dollar a week. The movie cost 16 cents, plus I needed a nickel for a box of DOTS. Then, of course, it was five cents here and five cents there for ice cream cones, Cokes, and other necessities, which mounted up each week and always left me destitute long before the next allowance day.

Secondly, I felt supreme confidence. I knew of three women who "liked" me—a veritable harem. Why shouldn't I meet Irene inside after she had bought her ticket, thereby saving 16 cents and a possible five cents more if she, for some reason, expected me to buy her candy? Sex was important, but I simply could not justify spending 42 cents—almost half my allowance—on one date.

Finally, I was unsure about what to say to her. What do you talk about with a girl? By meeting inside the theater, the need for conversation would be minimized.

Anyway, The Date was not about conversation. It was about physical attraction. Sex. Sitting in a dark theater with a woman. Letting nature take its course.

I usually attended the Saturday matinee with my sister. I told her I would go with her that week, but I wouldn't sit with her in the theater because I had a date.

"A date?" she said. "You?"

"Yes."

"This I have to see."

I spent the rest of the week selecting my outfit. I remember the shirt. It was two-tone, brown on the bottom and tan on top, with tan cuffs. There was red piping on the cuffs and across the middle of the back and the chest. It was stylish in a western sort of way. And what could be more appropriate for watching two cowboy movies?

My sister and I bought our tickets at the booth outside the front of the theater. "Where's your date?" she asked.

"I'm meeting her inside."

"You've got to be kidding." My sister turned and marched into the theater.

Then, at two p.m. on June 20, 1954, my first date began.

My timing was perfect. I waited outside the theater for a few more minutes, and then I stopped at the candy counter to buy a box of DOTS. Just as the lights were lowered, I found Irene in the darkening theater and sat next to her just as the movie began.

That memorable afternoon we sat together and watched two Roy Rogers movies, a newsreel, a Superman episode, and three cartoons.

I never spoke. Neither did Irene. I turned my head and looked at her a couple times, but our eyes never met. Our elbows did touch on the shared armrest a couple of times. I ate all the DOTS myself.

At five p.m. we walked together out of the theater and into the bright afternoon sunlight. My sister was waiting. Irene ran over to join Susie and Margie, and the three of them ran off jumping, squealing, and all talking at once.

"How was the date?" my sister asked.

"Great!"

I considered it a success, although Irene and I never dated again. I guess you could say we broke up. But I will not forget that first date. I can see her profile in the flickering light and feel the touch of her elbow.

It's hard to explain.

There was a real sexual, sensual thrill just sitting next to her.

That was all.

That was enough.

I don't know if it was as good for her as it was for me.

Maybe not.

Women are hard to figure.

SCENES FROM A WIDOWER'S LIFE

THE morphine had been increased to the point where she just slept. Bill took hold of her bony hand and squeezed it. It was limp but warm. "I'm here," he said, even though she probably could not hear him. The nurse Bill had hired stuck her head into the doorway. "Mary, why don't you go home tonight. There's no reason for you to stay."

"Thanks, Bill, but I'll be downstairs, just in case. I'll keep the TV on low. Call me if you need to get some sleep."

Mildred lay so still. They had spent the last month planning a cruise they would never take. The brochure was still on the bedside table—a small ship—eighteen days on the Mediterranean. She'd asked him if he'd made the required deposit. He lied and said he had. It would have been silly. He told her he'd reserved the best cabin on the ship.

At dawn Mary came back up the stairs. "We better call the funeral home," Bill said. He stood and turned to face her. They put their arms around each other and wept.

Living alone was hard. He taught himself to cook a few things, but he did it just because he had to eat. He liked a clean house. Mildred had kept it spotless, but he didn't clean. He didn't know how, except maybe to vacuum, so he had to hire someone, but he hated it when she was there banging around. She didn't seem to like him very much either. Mildred had always been clicking around upstairs, doing whatever she did. It used to irritate him, but he would have given anything if he could hear those sounds again.

What he did do was throw himself back into the business. In the little cubicle he had reserved for himself when he turned the business over to Steve, he found the contract he was looking for and printed it. He entered his old office, sat on the edge of his son's desk, and waited for a phone call to end. After a full five minutes, his son finally hung up. "Everything okay, Dad?" he asked.

"Yep," said Bill. "I have to talk to you about the new McPhearson contract. I thought we were going to talk about it yesterday, but you weren't here."

"I was working at home, Dad—fewer interruptions." Steve turned in his chair so his back was to his father, then he turned again—as if for effect—faced him, and folded his hands in front of him. "Dad, I don't want to talk about the contract."

"Just listen for a minute, Steve."

Steve held up his hand. "Dad, we did talk about the McPhearson contract. You need to let it go. Everyone worked hard on it, and I made the final decision. You need to let me succeed or fail on my own."

Bill glanced at the contract in his hand. "I understand, Steve, and as soon as this transition period is over..."

"It's been three years, Dad." Steve stepped around the desk and put his arm around his father's shoulder. "I decided we've transitioned." He smiled. "You know what you should do? You should take a cruise. Why not? You and Mom always talked about doing it."

Bill stood and returned to his cubicle. He couldn't take a cruise by himself.

Bill went fishing with his grandson Charlie, a sophomore at Holy Cross. "So how's Jenny?" asked Bill.

Charlie didn't answer right away. He was rummaging around in his tackle box. "That's over, Grandpa. She met some guy."

Bill gazed across the water as the rowboat slowly rocked on the waves. He and Mildred had thought that Jenny was perfect for Charlie. They'd started dating in eighth grade. "I'm sorry," said Bill.

"It's okay, Grandpa. I've already had some dates. I'm doing fine. How about you? Are you holding up?"

Bill could not tell his grandson how hopelessly lost he was or that this was the only pleasant day he had spent since the doctor had told them Mildred would die. He could not tell his grandson that, a few days before, the bartender at the Hyatt had told him to go home only to awaken the next morning inside his car in the garage with the engine still running. He couldn't be sure if it was lucky or unlucky that he hadn't killed himself. So he told his grandson, "I'm doing great, Charlie."

Before Bill met Mildred there was Flora. When he met Mildred, Flora was at Michigan, hundreds of miles away and, anyway, he was afraid to face her in person, so he broke up with his high school sweetheart over the phone. She kept asking, "What? What are you saying?" The connection wasn't bad, but the message was. Finally, she said, "Don't tell me it's over. I'll decide when it's over." He kept talking, but she stopped listening. Finally, she hung up. That was fifty years ago. Bill never saw her, never even talked to her in all those years, but he kept track, friends kept track and told him about Flora. Bill knew she had married and had kids and that her husband had died and that her kids were kind of jerks. She'd had a pretty good life, but it was kind of sad too. Anyway, he never thought of her. Well, he thought of her, but it was always Mildred. Yet, when Charlie told him about Jenny, Bill thought of

Flora again. Still, it took him six more months to work up the nerve to call her.

Flora lived less than a hundred miles away in Bristol in a big white house with a lot of lawn. The house was amazingly clean and neat. "What took you so long?" she wondered.

It was noon, so they went to lunch. They ran into a friend of Flora's who said, "So this is Bill. Well, I'm so glad you're here," as if he'd been expected.

It was awkward. All he could think of was Mildred. All he could feel was guilt. He'd forgotten how Flora was coarser than Mildred. It was Mildred's way to always make him feel in charge and at ease. With Flora there was some sort of tension, like they were in some kind of contest.

But then he realized they were exactly where they had been before Mildred, an intimacy they had recaptured almost without effort. Of course, it was not the same as Mildred, but it was better than the loneliness. He stayed three days.

Later, Flora came to stay with Bill. A week before the wedding, he came down to breakfast. Flora set a plate of bacon and eggs in front of him, served herself, and sat across the table from Bill. "I'm picking your tux up at the dry cleaner's today," she said. "I found your tie, cummerbund, and studs right where you put them, and I'll wash and press your formal shirt myself with all those damn pleats. How much starch?"

"The studs were where Mildred put them, which is why I couldn't find them," said Bill, "and no starch. Boy, what a lot of fuss for nothing."

"Nothing?" said Flora. "Your granddaughter getting married is not nothing. It's a milestone, and you are so lucky, Bill. You are blessed."

"I know. I know," said Bill, who had been playing the wedding down. He didn't want Flora to get all maudlin again over her own family's situation.

Bill could not believe the outfit—a dress to go fishing?

Charlie was waiting for them down by the dock, and Bill didn't care what Flora was wearing. She looked nice, and it was a chance for her and Charlie to get to know each other. It was not dawn yet, although there was some light. The whole sky was red. The sun would be coming up any minute. It would be a hot day, but it was still cold before the dawn. The only sounds were the birds. Bill was in his bare feet and old khakis. In addition to the dress, Flora wore a yellow silk scarf and matching yellow shoes that would be filthy before she even got into the boat.

As they gingerly stepped onto the dock from the muddy shoreline, a flock of birds unexpectedly rose in unison from a sycamore tree, dipping, then rising like a wave. The sunlight from below the horizon bounced off them like a thousand blinking lights. "Did you ever see anything so amazing?" asked Flora. Bill and Charlie made no comment. Breaking the awkward silence, Flora asked, "Am I overdressed?"

"You're fine," said Bill. Charlie smiled.

"Where's the boat?" she asked.

"Right here," said Bill.

"This thing?" said Flora, looking down at the rowboat with the old ten-horse Evinrude. As they set out across the water toward the dawn, Flora talked more about the birds and how she'd never been fishing before, but she didn't get a response, so she shut up.

An hour later Bill said, "How's college going?"

"Great, Grandpa, just great," said Charlie. "You bet."

The day seemed longer than usual even though it ended early because Flora "had to pee." While Flora was in the wooden shed at the dock that was generously called the bathroom, Bill and Charlie stood together pissing on the roots of a willow. "Does she always talk so much?" asked Charlie.

"No, she's just nervous. The family makes her nervous. You were real nice to her today, Charlie. Real nice. I appreciate that."

"I wonder if she got her wedding outfit and her fishing outfit confused."

Bill laughed. "Be interesting to see what she shows up in. Might be fancier than the bride."

Charlie laughed. "So, she's coming?"

"Why do you ask?"

"Haven't you talked to Aunt Susie?"

"No, why?"

"She's having a fit," said Charlie. Bill did not respond. He looked at Charlie, and Charlie shrugged his shoulders. "Grandpa, cheer up. Let's just the two of us go fishing next time."

"Great idea, Charlie—I'd love that—next Saturday."

"Isn't that the wedding?"

"Oh, yeah," said Bill. "The Saturday after that for sure. It's a date."

Bill was in bed, reading the *Wall Street Journal*, waiting for Flora, who was in the dressing room. She appeared, not in a nightgown but a flowing blue dress. "Well," she said, twirling, "what do you think?"

He pushed his glasses down his nose. "You're not sleeping in that?"

"No, silly, this is for the wedding. I got it yesterday. Cost a fortune. I'm so excited for Millie. I had such a nice long chat with her. And her Norman is such a nice boy. I'm so happy for them."

Bill smiled. The dress was not bad. He went back to his paper, and she returned in fifteen minutes in a nightgown. Her fragrance filled the room. It had been so many years, but he thought he could remember it from before he met Mildred. Flora slid under the sheet next to him and put a hand inside his pajama top. The newspaper was on his lap.

"You okay, Bill? Is something bothering you?"

"No, nothing."

"Thanks for taking me fishing. I enjoyed that. Especially when those birds flew out. Wasn't that something?" Bill kept reading. "Your grandson doesn't talk much, does he?"

"Oh, I wouldn't say that."

Bill's daughter, Susie, and her daughter, Millie, the bride, stopped by Monday morning. Millie left with Flora to do "a little shopping." Susie stayed to talk to her father. They sat on Bill's patio next to the pool. "Daddy, we need to talk about Flora." Bill drummed his fingers on the glass table. "It's less than a week until the wedding, and she seems to be under the impression that she's invited."

"She's not?"

"Daddy, it's less than two years since Mom died. Mom is going to be a very big part of this occasion. Her spirit will be there."

Bill stood and moved to the edge of the pool, his back to his daughter. "It's been more than two years. And we discussed this, Susie. I asked your permission. Not that I need it, but I did ask."

There was silence, and Bill wondered if his daughter would say anything more. She did. "What you said, Daddy, was that you are having a terrible time getting over Mom. You asked me if it would be inappropriate if you talked to a friend—no, not even a friend—a widow going through the same thing. I didn't realize it was your old girlfriend, and she was going to move in and sleep in Mom's bed." Bill turned and faced her. Father and daughter should not discuss such a thing. They did sleep in the same bed and share the bathroom. It wasn't sex. They touched. It was a relationship, or something. He didn't know what it was. It didn't seem right that she should sleep in Susie's room. "So, Daddy, just what are your plans with Flora?"

"Please, let's not go there, Susie," said Bill, who had no plans.

"Okay, Daddy, we won't go there, but just where is it we are going? I'm going crazy. That's where I'm going."

"Susie, I'm your father, not your child."

She sighed. He started for the house.

"Daddy, wait. We have to discuss this. We have to discuss the wedding. Nothing else, okay?" Bill turned back to face her. "Millie doesn't want her there."

"Really?"

"Yes."

"Susie, I find that hard to believe. And Flora has a new dress she bought just for the wedding. She showed it off to me. Twirled around like a schoolgirl. She's all excited for Millie. And Millie likes her. I mean, you know, they just went off shopping together. You know I've told you that Flora's own daughter hasn't spoken to her in years. I'm sorry. I just can't do this to Flora."

"Well, Dad, I'm just telling you. You know Millie would never say anything to you. You know that." Bill turned and headed for the house, leaving his daughter sitting by the pool.

In the bedroom the new dress was draped over the bed with some scarves of various colors that Millie and Flora had brought back from their shopping excursion. He picked up the scarves and, one at a time, tried to match them to the dress. He was amazed at how soft and light they were. They were like picking up air. Flora emerged from the bathroom in her slip, and he turned with a pink scarf in one hand and a scarf of some pastel color he could not name in the other. "Which one do you like?" she asked.

He studied the scarves in his hands, then sat on the edge of the bed. "Flora, there's something we need to talk about. I'm really sorry for waiting so long, but we've got to talk about it." Flora had moved to the closet, her back toward him. She was holding three diamond-studded necklaces up to the neckline of her slip and looking in the mirror. She didn't turn around, but she was only a few feet away, so he knew she had heard him, so he kept talking. "Well, I've been thinking, Flora. I mean, you know, widows remarry all the time, and so do men. Whatever. But no one gets another mother. You lose your mother, and there's just a hole—a hole you can't fill."

He glanced up to see that Flora had turned to face him, hands on hips, a diamond necklace in her hand. "Is this speech about me and the wedding? If it is, you can forget it. I'm not an idiot. I know what's going on, and it's not about me. It's about your daughter, who happens to be a spoiled brat." Then she returned to her task, putting all but one diamond necklace away, and placing the one she had chosen next to the dress on the bed. Then she turned to Bill and said, "I suppose you were going to tell me that Millie doesn't want me to come, which is a load of horse crap, and you know it." She took the pastel scarf from his hand and placed it on her dress. "And your son is no prize either." He handed her the pink scarf, and she walked away. "End of discussion," she said from inside the closet.

The summer evening was so pleasant as they sat together on the glider on the screened-in porch. Cicadas filled the air with their buzzing, and now and then a warm breeze slipped through.

"Baseball great Mel," said Flora, "three letters."

"Ott," said Bill, "Mel Ott."

"Here's one I know you only see in crossword puzzles," said Flora, "Oriental nurse."

"Amah," said Bill.

"How did you know that?"

"Mildred and I used to do these puzzles, just like this, sitting right here."

Flora put the puzzle in her lap. Bill felt a choking sensation, and he didn't know if he could even speak. He put his head down and sat quietly for a minute, and then he said, "Give me another clue." He leaned against Flora and put his arm around her, but he turned his face away so she couldn't see it.

"Okay," she said, "ancient city on the Euphrates—six letters—no, wait, seven letters."

"That's so easy," said Bill. "Cleveland."

"Good for you," said Flora, filling in the squares. "I'll just shorten it a little so it fits."

"Let me see that," said Bill, grabbing the puzzle. "Babylon? You sure it's not Cleveland?" He handed it back.

Bill set the *Wall Street Journal* on his pillow, put his hands on his knees, pulled himself up, and went into the bathroom to brush his teeth. When he returned, the lights were out. Flora was lying with her back to him. He slid under the covers next to her but kept to his side of the bed.

"Bill," she said, "I've decided that, after the wedding, I'm going home."

He shifted onto his back and stared up into the darkness.

At three a.m., on schedule, he got up to go to the bathroom.

In the bathroom, lit only by the nightlight, he stared into the mirror and observed his dark silhouette surrounded by a soft glow. He wished he had taken Susie in his arms and told her that he understood how much she missed her mother. Why couldn't he tell Flora that she should not go to the wedding—for Susie's sake? Why hadn't he told his son that he needed to be involved in the business, just involved? Why couldn't he tell anyone how lonely he was? When he used to be afraid of things at the office, he would tell Mildred, and she would hold him, and the sound of her voice was all he needed. She had held everything together. Now, she was gone.

"What on earth are you doing in there?" said Flora from the bed.

He came back and lay quietly next to her, breathing softly. "Flora?" he said.

"What?"

"May I go with you?"

"Of course you can. Now go to sleep."

PUBLICATION CREDITS

The stories in this collection were copyrighted by the author and first published, as follows, in the following Literary Journals:

"An Artist in the Family" - Hawaii Pacific Review 12/30/2015, "The Birds of Bristol Court" - Crack the Spine 2013 – also accepted for Spring 2014 print anthology - "The Bull" - Riddle Fence 1/11/2014 – "Circus City" - Jelly Bucket 1/20/2019, Poydras Review 11/6/2018, Blue Lake Review 9/25/2018, "Edith's Summer" - Gulf Stream 4/25/2013, Stickman Review Vol 12 N 1, 2013, Amarillo Bay 2/7/2013, "Family" - Voices De La Luna 8/5/2019, "The Filmmaker and the Night Watchman" - Valparaiso Fiction Review 11/24/2015, "Ghosts in the House" - Door is a Jar Magazine 7/27/2020 – "The Goldfish with

Long Black Hair" - Qwerty 10/14/2016, Griffin 2/17/2016, "In Which Walt Weighs 300 Pounds and Cindy Has Sex with the Pool Boy" - Diverse Voices Quarterly 8/18/2015, Saint Ann's Review 3/25/2015, "Kaplan's Furniture Store" - OxMag 10/18/2016, Verdad 10/18/2016, "The Liberation" - New Orleans Review 11/10/2008, "Marilee" - Forge Journal 2/8/2013, PANK Magazine 10/7/2012, "Maureen and Sylvia" - Wild Violet 2/9/2013, "Morgan the Plumber" - North Dakota Quarterly 4/28/2012, "Women Are Hard to Figure" - Legendary 7/19/2011, "Scenes from a Widower's Life" - Sanskrit 1/13/2014, MacGuffin 11/8/2013, Write Room 8/9/2013

ABOUT THE AUTHOR

PETER Obourn was born in 1941, in a small industrial Village in upstate New York. "I barely remember the war, but postwar, coming of age in the 50s was incredible—tail fins, television, Elvis, Ike, poodle skirts . . . " After a successful career as a lawyer/businessman, he began his life as a struggling writer, and has found the writer's life a great deal more difficult than law or business. But he is philosophical about it. "If people would just read my damn stories . . . " he says.

After attending a multitude of creative writing retreats, he proudly received a Master of Fine Arts degree from Lesley University in Cambridge. Despite his struggles, his award winning fiction and poetry have been published in many literary journals, including one Pushcart Prize nomination.

He and his wife Linda, who have two children and

four grandchildren, now reside in the hamlet of Egypt, New York and summer on a quiet lake in the Adirondack Mountains near Old Forge. He is at work on several novels, a little woodworking and his backhand.

He has a website – peterobourn.com

MIKE Kielkopf is an award-winning writer, editor, and teacher who has published thousands of articles and six books, edited millions of words, and taught in high schools and colleges around the world. He holds an MA from the University of Iowa, and he and his wife Mary, also an Iowa grad, are based in Waterloo, Iowa.

COMING SOON: And once you've lived this series of short stories, be on the lookout for another journey through the power of a mama's words: *"Holcomb, there's a difference between being foolish and having hope. Never lose hope."*

Discover how one mother's wisdom plays out as Peter Obourn takes you on an entrancing exploration of human nature in his new novel, *Holcomb's Potato Song*, planned to be published soon.

Made in the USA
Middletown, DE
10 October 2021